This is a solid, fact-based story, about a Ren Faire actor who loses his best friend under very suspicious circumstances. When no one else will, he begins to investigate-- and rapidly learns that the best of intentions can get you seriously hurt when you go up against a remorseless killer. Villains galore, lots of action, realistic fight scenes and strong characterization makes this worth reading. The fencing scenes happened just as written, and it is good to see someone get it right.

'The real 'Jillian' of the story.....

I0548062

Faire,
Foul
and
Fatal

Teel
James
Glenn

GORDIAN KNOT BOOKS

Dedication

To Janis who has stayed the course when others have disappeared.

Acknowledgments

Joan, Sharon and Joy, who were the first guides along the path that ended in this book as it is now. Thank you.

Foreword

This is not a book about death, though death is part of it.

This is not a book about memories, though the memories are so strong they compelled its writing.

This is not about the man I call Tom, but rather about the changes he and his murder wrought in me. That being so, many will still say it is a book about death.

Not so.

It is a book about life and the people who make it worth living: the love they give and the joy they leave behind.

I wish I didn't have to write it, and if the real Tom were here (and he knows why), I'd wring his scrawny neck. But until we cross blades again on the other side, this one's for him. And for the real Jillian, who has had the courage to survive and to prosper.

Prologue

The rain pattered insistently against the tent above my head and the wind howled like a lost soul but all I was really aware of was that I had a man's blood on my hands.

The blood of the man I had killed.

I could not see them clearly in the darkness of the tent, but I could feel the warm sticky mess dripping down my arms and drying on me along with the mud that was crusting on my clothes.

My side ached so bad I wanted to cry out, but I had no strength left to even moan.

All I could do was sit in numbed silence listening to the *rat-tat-tat* of the rain on the canvas above me while I waited for the police to come and take me away.

I tried to think of how it all got to there, to make some sense of it and try and figure out how so much had happened since that day in the schoolyard.

Most of all I, thought about Tom.

Chapter One

The point of the sword was coming in fast at my middle with a hundred and fifty pounds of thrust behind it so I had little time to do anything but react. I hopped back on both feet like a matador and brought my own rapier over the top with force in a circular parry. His point was knocked out of line and missed me by three inches.

It was enough.

Before he could recover from his deep lunge, I sprang off my left foot into a demi-lunge of my own, intending to drag my rapier blade along his belly.

Obviously, he had a different program planned.

He lunged with his right leg forward, with his left leg unusually far back, and his left hand held out to the side in what I thought was sloppy form. Wrong! He smoked me again.

As I placed my weight on my forward leg going for the belly cut, he dropped onto his left forearm and, using his left leg as a brace, kicked out with his right to sweep my exposed front leg from underneath me.

Bang! I landed with my full two hundred fifty pounds on my right hip. My sword went flying and he was on me.

"Where the hell is that in Agrippa?" I asked as I pulled off my fencing mask. Tom De Dannin removed his mask, laughing so hard he had to pull out his inhaler and suck some air.

"I stole that move from the Jackie Chan movie we saw last month in Chinatown," he said. "You ought to know it. I think I'll call it the Tom D. trip!" He grinned, that infectious Irish grin of his again. I had no choice but to laugh at myself and accept his proffered hand to again stand on my feet.

Just another of our weekly workouts in the schoolyard in Bay Ridge in 1997.

Tom, aside from the legitimate fencing training he'd had, was a scrapper with bits and pieces of four martial arts under his skinny belt and a lot of bar fights behind him. I always tried out my choreographic ideas with him and often profited from his knowledge. It was worth limping home every once in a while.

"You just don't have the killer instinct, Eric," he said as we walked back to the Gatorade and our gear. He set down the theatrical rapier he had used to beat me and picked up his personal one. He'd named the sword Courage and he took great delight in flourishing it to heighten the shame of my defeat. "All this theatrical stuff has taken off your edge combat edge besides warping your mind."

"Another fall like that and it'll warp my back beyond repair. Ow!"

"No pain, no gain."

"I like the one about 'Get my stunt double or I'm quitting this picture' better! Remember all *my* adventures are fake!"

"Stunt double in a pig's eye," Tom said as he adjusted his ratty black beret so that his "Free Ireland" pin was positioned over his right eye. "You know that most of the wimp actors can't handle the genuine article in even a staged fight." He slashed the air with sharp-edged Courage, making an ominous *swash* sound. "It'd make you nuts to see some stunt man screw up a fight you know you can do a thousand times better!"

"Well, all this stuff is gonna come out in better choreography for some of those 'wimp actors' at the Renaissance faire this year," I said. "I'm gonna blow that artistic director's socks off. I'll give 'em a little taste at the Cloisters next week, then, come August...!"

"Best showcase for your fight choreography yet, huh?" He swilled down the last of a Coke he'd left by our gear. He seemed able to drink more Coke than should have been able to fit into his skinny frame and never sloshed!

"Yeah, people notice the choreographer on this faire, I've been assistant two years running. Now, with Steve gone and him putting in

4 • Teel James Glenn

a good word for me, it's finally my show. Joust, human chess match and the highwayman scenes. It'll be a living resume and get my name around on the circuit."

"Don't let it go to your head, big guy, I can still kick your butt in a real fight."

"I'll fight you anywhere, anytime," I said with a Sergio Leone pause as I cast a sinister glance from head to toe of his skinny five-ten frame. "Anytime … as long as it's choreographed, and I'll look good whipping you." I stretched to my full six-foot-six frame and made a muscle builder pose.

He laughed hard.

Then he got a serious, almost dreamy look on his face. "We were both born at least five centuries too late, man." He sat with his back against the wall of the handball court, an unlit cigarette dangling almost magically from his bottom lip.

"Sometimes, I think I was born in the wrong century, too," I said, taking a big gulp from the Gatorade bottle, "but then again, I kind of like antibiotics and color TV."

"Don't be a total hairbag, man," he said affectionately. His voice still had a Baltimore twang that his years in New York had barely softened. "I know neither of us would have made it in Sparta—asthma and all the allergies we got—but, hell." His blue eyes sharpened focus on some place other than a schoolyard in Bay Ridge, Brooklyn. "Don't you feel it sometimes, Eric, especially at a Medieval Society event or a Renaissance faire? Like you're just gonna walk around a corner and be home, with a sword on your hip, living by your wits and skill in a world where our word means something, and so does the next guy's. Honor, chivalry! Where there just might be a dragon over the horizon, or at least, a dragon ship."

I laughed. "And you say Jillian is the poet in the family."

"I'm Irish," he said grinning his ten-dollar smile. "Rhyming and roguishness come with the genes." He pushed off the wall and to his feet, at the same time filching the Gatorade jug out of my hand. "Let's get this stuff inside and get some pizza and Coke."

I picked up the masks, bokkens and rubber knives. Tom grabbed the epee-bladed stage swords, a towel we used as a cloak, and his

4

Courage. Even though the blade on Courage was sharp, he always brought it along to practice solo forms and as a good luck charm.

"More Coke? So much for flagons, dragons and wild boar."

As we crossed Thirty-Sixth Street he said, "It'd be a fair trade. Nowadays, Arthur's, Chuhulain's, and Siegfried's only chances to be heroes would be to give up a seat on the R train to an old woman."

"Yeah, no Beau Geste for us, no ballads. If we make it to Avalon, it'll be by public transit."

"It'd be a dull place to go," Tom said. "I always hoped for Valhalla—Irish blood notwithstanding."

"Well the way things are going in the world," I said, more than a little serious, "we might just be around for the Viking version of the big bang: Ragnarok."

"I hope not." He pushed against the wrought iron and glass foyer door. "Who'll build the funeral ships for us and put the dog at our feet for our Viking funeral?"

"Be a bitch to hitch hike to Valhalla, huh?"

"Damn, straight!" He laughed. "Especially considering I never learned to swim!"

Chapter Two

When we arrived upstairs at their apartment, Tom's wife, Jillian, was waiting for us with cold Cokes and a hot lecture. "I hope you two were having fun," she scolded. "I've been up here sorting clothes for two hours while you boys played 'Errol Flynn.'"

"We weren't playing," Tom said. "I *was* Errol Flynn!"

"And with this honker," I added in the voice of Captain Levasseur from *Captain Blood*, "I was Basil Rathbone."

Jill tried to stay mad, but with the two of us being so damn charming she just managed a dismissive wave of her hand. She stood five foot four with orange-red hair cut shoulder length, pale clear skin, and eyes greener than Ireland.

Their apartment looked as if an aspiring fantasy writer-librarian and a history nut lived there, which was good enough shorthand for the two of them. Books covered every flat surface and had begun to organically grow out of the bookcases that filled most of the walls. Posters made from blow-ups of book covers and a science fiction convention poster I had drawn that had a portrait of Jillian on it filled the rest of the available wall space.

That was how I'd met the two of them, and it didn't feel like three years had passed since then. Jill and I had been on a panel together at a science fiction convention—I was doing more book illustration back then. Jill and I began talking about British fantasy writers. Tom was there too. He and I somehow got onto Renaissance sword styles. And the three of us spent the whole weekend in one long rambling conversation that kept on afterward pretty much non-stop since then.

Our original trio had since grown to a floating dozen or so who called ourselves "The Company of the Silver Swan," after the little newsletter we all contributed to (and Jill edited) which was, in turn, named after the pub in which we had first started meeting.

"You want one plain and one with mushrooms and sausage, as usual or are you feeling adventurous?" Jill queried.

Both of us grunted affirmatively, and Jill punched the speed dial function on the phone labeled "Pizza." It was a wonder there wasn't a pneumatic service tube directly to Lenny's Pizzeria. She ordered one plain and one with everything; heartburn be damned.

Corwin the Cat, named after the main character in *Nine Princes in Amber*, wandered into the room to check out the noise. He was a long-haired, regal black, and we were all sure he had been a fashion model in his former life. He made a beeline for allergic me, and Tom deflected him with a faked sidekick. Their other cat, Pyewacket, lounged dopily on the windowsill.

"Robin called while you two were outside," Jill said quietly. "She went ahead and filed. Looks like she's split from Danny for good this time."

We all exchanged a look that said we were thinking the same thing: How long would it be *this time* until she went back to him? Robin Madden and Dan her husband, had gone through several breakups, well documented in her autobiographical letters to the Silver Swan newsletter. It was particularly messy because she had a five-year-old son by Danny. We had all sort of adopted little Danny, who despite all the sturm and drang was a pretty well-adjusted kid. She wasn't very strong about being alone, even though it was clear it would be best for all of them at this point.

The silence hung heavy 'til Jill broke it with a great deflection shot. "I guess we won't see much of you once you start rehearsals for the faire, huh, Eric?" I smiled at her and grabbed a straw.

"We have the first fight rehearsal tomorrow, and with the shorter rehearsal period Dawn and Barry are giving me this year, it looks like you're gonna have to give Tom a workout yourself for a month or so."

Tom choked on a gulp of soda. "Oh no, don't tell her that," he said with a tone of abject horror in his voice. "I use our workouts in the park as an excuse to get out of my matrimonial duties."

He absent-mindedly reached for Courage, brandishing the swept-hilt rapier as if it were a talisman to protect his purity. Jillian had given it to him on his twenty-first birthday. He hadn't named it until later when he'd worn it at their wedding, as he clung for dear life to the hilt all through the ceremony. It didn't work then either; she still got him!

"Now, you've got no excuse." Jill giggled as she leaned over Tom's shoulder, snatched the sword from him and whispered in his ear. "I guess we'd better pick up some vitamins on the way home from work tomorrow." Tom tried hard to look as if it was a horrid prospect. He failed miserably and we all broke up in belly laughs.

"That reminds me, do you guys still have to be in housing court next week?"

"Yeah, don't remind me, I just want to be done dealing with this landlord." He got up and headed toward the bathroom, mumbling all the way.

"He's dreaded housing court for weeks," she said quietly. "Too many authority figures."

I suppressed a very unmanly giggle.

"Once we confront that shit landlord with all the check stubs, we'll get all this straightened out, and then he can relax."

"He's been edgy lately," I said seriously, "more than an eviction notice should warrant."

"It just made him mad as sin at that old, avaricious so-and-so. We'll beat him in court once we show the repair bills and check stubs."

"Any idea why he's been so edgy?" I was cleaning the glasses in the sink and almost dropped mine when she spoke.

"I'm pretty sure it's that damned SAS man," she said.

"SAS?" I asked. "As in British Special Air Services—shoot 'em and run boys?"

Jill gave a disgusted snort in agreement. "Some guy approached Tom at a lunch counter near the printing plant and offered to sell him machine guns for the IRA."

I stared at her, truly stunned. I knew both she and Tom wanted, and had worked peacefully, to get the British out of Northern Ireland. While Tom might like a good mano-a-mano brawl, they both had always told me they abhorred the senseless violence of the gunfire and bombs.

"You're not serious, Jill?"

"That's what I said to Tom, but—"

"I damn sure am," Tom said, returning to the room with a wide grin on his evil leprechaun face.

"Since when do you fuck around with guns?" I asked.

"I don't," he said, "but that SAS hairbag didn't know that."

"Did he tell you he's SAS?"

"No, he said he was a Provo-sympathizer, and he'd 'heard' I was real active in the cause. He said he heard about the relief drive we organized last fall and all that."

"So?" I did a John Wayne with my hands on my hips and tried to stare him down.

"So, this Mister Thomas Gunns (hah!) said he knew a guy who could lay his hands on one hundred MAC-10s and all the ammo I could use."

"Geez!" My John Wayne went south in favor of a Jerry Lewis take.

"We had lunch a couple of times and he just smelled wrong." Tom gave a gleeful little chuckle. "So I figured this 'Tommy' was either SAS or FBI—you know, trying to set me up for a sting."

"And why didn't you let me in on any of this?"

"I wanted to wait until I had an ending." He grinned. "You see, man, I figured I'd sting him. I talked to that Wop sergeant I know—"

"Perisi?"

"Yeah, Tony Perisi. He's an okay guy, but I know he's bucking for a promotion. A catch like that would be a feather in his hat. So I told him—oh sweet, innocent me—about this big bad 'Provo,' and he tells me to get samples or some concrete info so he can call in some ATF boys to bust Mr. Provo."

"So?" I sat down, stunned by his real-life brush with adventure.

"So, *pffft!*" He threw up his hands and shrugged. "I guess he either found out I filed a report or just got edgy himself. The contact number

9

I got for him was disconnected. Nothing for three weeks now, so I figure he's split."

"You two-faced Irish James Bond," I chided him. "You had every actor's dream scenario going on and you held out on me!" I shook a fist at him. "That's it—Jill gets a comp, but you pay to see me at the Faire!"

Tom was about to make some witty, sarcastic reply when the door buzzer announced the pizza. A half hour of serious consumption and silly jokes followed.

It was the closest I can imagine to heaven sitting in the messy living room giggling like pre-teens with the two of them. There was no sense that there was anything really bad in the world, that as long as the pizza parlors of the world were open and there was a sword brother like Tom or a bard like Jillian in my life there would never be a shadow I could not dodge.

After the "sacred" circle of pizza was consumed we started to clean up for me to get on my way.

"Do you still want to borrow that chainmail coif for the Cloisters show tomorrow?" Jill asked.

"Right!" I answered as I put the leftover soda in the fridge.

I was doing a promotional for the faire at the one-day event at the Cloisters Museum in Manhattan the next day and was going to use Tom's headpiece to supplement my costume.

Jillian rummaged around in their hall closet and produced a canvas sack. It held the aluminum head coif and a leather arming cap that went beneath it to prevent the chainmail links from pulling my hair out.

"Are you doing a joust or just a tilt at lunch time?" Tom asked.

"Tilt at one and tilt and ground fight at five o'clock. D and B were too cheap to spring for training time with the faire horses or much rehearsal time for us."

"You and the cowboy?" Jill asked with a little wry grin. She loved the idea of a cowboy in armor.

"Yep," I laughed. "Good old Kelly and with Vita and Smitty on the ground. We're just going to recycle some stuff from last year on this one."

"We might not make the one o'clock one," Jill said with a slight pout. "We have a 'Free Ireland' picnic to go to, but we won't be very late."

"No sweat, hon, and no suspense. Kelly will win the tilt. He's the one who can really ride. I just sit on the horse until somebody knocks me off, which for some reason seems to be every joust!" I finished cleaning up the meal. Jill grabbed the last of her laundry, and Tom packed my swords and the chainmail beanie for me into my duffle bag.

"So, like I started to ask before, do you guys still want me to watch the apartment a week from Monday when you're at court?"

"We don't want you to take time off from the health club or the Ren faire," Jill said.

"I took a month sabbatical from the club to get the Faire going," I smiled seriously, "and I already scheduled a day off for a 'doctor's appointment.'"

"You are a gem!" Without thinking she leaned over and hugged me.

As with any time she and I touched, it was a stiff sort of contact. It was because both of us were very aware of the physical chemistry we refused to acknowledge.

Sarcastically, Tom grinned from where he stood by the door, completely aware of our discomfort. He found it a vast source of amusement. Theirs was an "open" sort of relationship, and technically Jill was free to "bed" anyone she chose (though it was an option she had never used). Tom trusted her and me to keep it just physical if anything happened. I'm not sure we trusted ourselves.

"I'll take the garbage out and tell José that Eric'll be watching the apartment next week and your cousin will be here tomorrow." Since they'd gotten the notice of the eviction proceeding three weeks previous, they always made sure someone was in the apartment at all times.

"When did Tom tell you about this gun runner thing?" I asked Jill after Tom went to see José.

"He told me right off," she said, dumping a bag of socks on the floor to sort through, "or I'd have killed him when I did finally find out."

"Et tu, Jillian?" I shook my head in disbelief. "Still, I'm surprised you didn't at least hint at it."

"He swore me to secrecy." She laughed. "He wanted so much to gloat to you about his adventure."

"He got me anyway. Even a near miss at adventure is better than the make-believe stuff I do for a living. Gods! What genius came up with a corny name like Tommy Gunns!"

Tom was back in a couple of minutes. "José wasn't home, I'll catch up with later."

"Well, I'd better roll out," I said. "I promised A.C. that I'd stop by. He's got a new Jackie Chan film for me to copy!" Tom gave a fist victory-salute in the air.

"Way to go, A.C.!"

"Well, give him a hello from us," Jill added. When she saw the look in Tom's eyes, she said, "And just one beer, Tom. Mandy's coming over later, and I want to clean up the place a bit."

"You bet, Boss! I'm gonna walk Eric to the train stop."

I kissed Jill goodbye on the forehead, then Tom and I headed out.

Two blocks later the two of us stood at the foot of the elevated train station waiting for a train to pull in. "This housing court appearance does have you spooked," I said. "It's not just the SAS loony toon."

"The idea of being in a building with so many blue suits I can't punch out gives me hives!" Tom's face was so serious that I broke out laughing. He looked real hurt for a moment, then added, "And I'm not so sure we can win against the landlord."

That drew me up short. "What do you mean?"

"He's right about some of our rent payments being late ... I, uh...." He looked like a puppy who'd wet on the carpet and been caught. "I played the horses a lot this last year. Jill doesn't know."

I stared at him. "Geez, Tom, how bad?"

"Oh, I'm paid up on the electric and phone, and only a month behind on the rent." He looked at his feet and kicked an imaginary stone. I suddenly felt like Andy doing a father and son talk with Opie.

12

"Once I was three months late on the rent," he continued. "That's when we got the notice."

"Okay, as long as you pay up I don't see how he can really evict you, even with all the battle you've had with him over the heating and that bad leak in the bathroom last year. If you need the last month's dough—"

"No," he cut me off. "I've got it with this last paycheck."

"So, call the guy, tell him there was a bank screw up and it won't happen again. Right?"

He didn't look convinced.

"You gonna tell Jill before she finds out in court?"

"Oh hell, Eric," Tom said. "I'd rather cut off my arm than disappoint Jill again!"

Tom had been a pretty wild street kid when he'd met Jill in Baltimore. Five years younger than her, he had to grow up real fast for her sake, and there'd been growing pains along the way. Some of which involved him screwing up; gang fights, some petty theft charges and he once punched out an undercover cop. Jill loved to tell that story. He was my friend, but he was no angel.

"Well, you need to tell her before the court hearing, just in case things don't go well. But I'll check with A.C. One of his senior students is a lawyer. If the landlord won't accept the check, I'll see what can be done."

"Thanks, man," Tom said drawing a deep breath. "I'll tell her tonight." He headed back to their apartment, and I yelled at him from the train platform.

"You better hide Courage before you do!" I grinned. "I'll talk to you during the week."

The N train ride was a little over an hour; elevated through Brooklyn, underground in Manhattan, and elevated again in Queens. I was in the midst of re-reading Arthur Wise's *The Art and History of Personal Combat* to crib ideas for the Faire so the time flew by.

I didn't have to pay too much attention to the trip because Ditmars, my stop, was at the end of the line. It allowed me to get lost in another time; rapiers and broadswords, colichemardes and cutlasses were like cotton candy to me. I had to agree with Tom. I often felt like I had been born in the wrong time and place and yet, with the Renaissance faire and the Shakespearean shows, I got my chance to time travel.

When the train jerked to a stop at the end of the line I looked up from the training schools of the Musketeers to glance across the platform directly in the second-floor window of Yum's Hwa Rang Do Academy of Queens, run by my friend, A.C. Black.

He was my Asian martial arts instructor and a good friend. We'd worked together playing thugs on a *Spenser for Hire* TV episode years ago. Our thugs insulted Hawk and were beaten up for our trouble. We both played lots of thugs. A.C. was even better at it than me; some might say he was a natural.

When I exited the train, I watched A.C. working the heavy bag at the far end of the room. He had a white t-shirt and kick pants on, and both were stuck to him with sweat, contrasting sharply with his mahogany-brown skin. He was working the bag methodically, arms and legs slamming into the canvas with such raw force I could almost feel it from where I stood. I could certainly remember how powerful they felt from sparring with him.

I watched for a few minutes, enjoying his technique. He wasn't the textbook definition of graceful, not at five ten and one hundred ninety pounds of ex-football player muscle, but there was an economy of force that was both beautiful and frightening to watch.

I hurried downstairs from the elevated platform to the street level entrance of the school between the pizza parlor and the candy store and used my key to let myself in. I climbed the stairs with my sword bag hanging heavy on my shoulder.

"Look what the cat dragged in," A.C. said when I bowed into the mat area of the dojang. He had a jump rope around his shoulders and was working with the six-inch hardwood Dan Bong, which was one of the unique weapons of Hwa Rang Do. It was used to strike nerve centers. A.C. was slow-motioning a form with the little Billy club, breathing evenly in a relaxed cooldown.

"Did you bring food?" he forced out between breaths.

"No, I didn't bring food." I dropped my shoulder pack, which contained almost all I owned. It seemed to be a phenomenon with most New Yorkers—we didn't have cars to cart out lives around with us; I swear, if I could get a sink in there I'd never have to go home.

I carried books, clothes, and repair parts for swords. Sometimes it outweighed my sword bag.

"But, oh noble master of the martial arts, I can go get food while you scrape off a few layers of slime if you so desire." I gave an exaggerated movie-style bow.

"Three slices with everything," he called as he skipped rope back toward the shower room, "And a bottle of cherry Coke."

"You're welcome," I yelled back on the way downstairs.

I got a chicken cutlet sandwich for myself along with his order; I eat like two horses, so sue me.

By the time I was back with the food, A.C. had showered and set up the VCR on the center of the mat. He'd lived in the tiny office at the back of the school for almost a year, since his divorce, and my two-room apartment was only ten blocks away, so we did regular movie nights.

"Let me put the screens up." He pulled Shoji screens in front of the windows so the view from outside was blocked and then settled down next to me and started the tape.

We ate in silence except for an occasional, "Oh my God, run that back!" to watch some incredible stunt or fight move. Gradually, we slipped in small talk. After a bit I told him about Tom's IRA near-adventure and landlord problem.

"I haven't seen that lawyer, Vinnie, in quite a while," A.C. said. "Some problem with his mother-in-law. But I can ask Poppo tomorrow. He's a housing cop; as a detective he should have pretty good idea where Tom and Jill sit in all this."

"Great. I'd love to give Tom some good news after he tells Jill." A.C. made a face.

"Wilma was bad," he said, invoking his ex-wife as if she were a creation of Dante's, "but as sweet as Jillian can be, I'd shoot myself before I'd tick off that Irish woman."

He held up his soda cup and toasted, "To ex-wives. May they get what they deserve!" We clinked paper cups and drained our sodas. The movie ended, and we started to clean up.

"Take the pizza boxes down when you go," A.C. said. "Grand Master is coming in to teach for me tomorrow night, and if he finds out I'm off kimchee and rice, he'll tan my hide."

Grand Master Yum oversaw teaching at five area schools and rotated visits to them all. He also took a personal interest in the health and appearance of all his black belts; he had decided A.C. needed to lose a little weight so had set him a diet. A.C. didn't do diets well.

"Aha," I said, gathering up all my gear and the food debris, "we have traded in a wife for a master-in-law, eh, Grasshopper?"

"You wait'll I get your butt in class tomorrow night," he called down the stairs after me. "I'll wear you down to my height."

"Don't you remember?" I smiled back. "My first day of rehearsal is Monday. Tomorrow it's me, Vita and Smitty at the Cloisters. I won't be in class most of this week." His brow wrinkled, and I could see his eyes narrow behind his glasses.

"Weasel!" he said. "Good luck!"

"'Night, Grasshopper."

He threw a towel at me and missed.

When I got home there were three messages on my answering machine—one from my mom in Florida, "Just calling to say hello," one from Red O'Boyle, the production stage manager from the Ren faire reminding me that my first rehearsal was Monday at ten a.m., and one from Smitty, the fight captain. "Hi, Eric, it's me, Smitty. I just called to let you know I finished the leather belt you wanted for your costume. I'm going out. I'll bring it tomorrow."

Great, I thought. *You are a gem, Smitty.*

I showered and stowed my gear in the hall closet, which I called my "armory." I looked around my two-room apartment thinking again that it looked like the "bad guys" had searched it. Once more, I decided to do nothing about it. Instead, I called my mom back to see how she was doing and chatted for a couple of minutes then made a phone call to Delaware but got the answering machine.

"You've reached five-five-five-two-oh-seven-five. Krystal is probably off showing Baryshnikov how it's done, so please leave your name and number at the sound of the beep."

"Hey, Kryss," I said into the receiver, "it's the big guy. I'm turning in early, got a big day tomorrow at the Cloisters Faire. I'm looking forward to seeing you in a couple of weeks. I miss your cute butt. Talk to you tomorrow night."

I unplugged the phone and set the alarm for nine before settling under the sheet. It was eleven ten.

I had a lot of nervous energy that I wished Kryss were close enough to take care of, but other than that, I remember thinking life wasn't half bad at all as I drifted off to sleep.

Chapter Three

The Cloisters Museum was made up of pieces of medieval buildings brought over from Europe, refitted together and plunked down in a park in northern Manhattan. It provided a beautiful view of the Hudson River and the wild New Jersey shore, kept wild in perpetuity by a far-sighted Rockefeller who bought the land and donated it for the medieval collection of the Metropolitan Museum of Art.

Displayed inside the impressive pseudo-castle were the Unicorn Tapestries, triptychs, and rosary bead nativities carved out of ivory, a knight's tomb, paintings, a medieval herb garden and lots of quiet stone walks and corridors I'd spent countless hours walking through. I always had a feeling I had gone home to an earlier time when I was there.

They also put on a free medieval faire one Sunday a year to help promote the collection. They used to hold it in the courtyard at the back, but it caught on and grew, so now it spilled out to the green fields around the building and along the long spiral path that wound up the hill it was built on.

The powers that be tried to make the faire "period" accurate since it was connected to an educational institution. In truth, however, the terms "medieval" and "renaissance" were treated interchangeably by the general public and the marketing worlds, making many a historian wince.

This one, though it called itself a medieval faire, was also a hybrid and the academic community of the museum has learned to live with it for the attention it brought the museum and the parks department. As for the public that swarmed to it, it was just a fun time, and the price was just right; free!

If you've never been to a Faire, it's a hard beastie to describe. Each is an experience that's decidedly more Hollywood than historical—picture part carnival, part flea market, part burlesque house and part Errol Flynn movie.

The rennies—as we who work on the Ren faire circuit call ourselves—are an odd assortment. A lot of rennies are old (or nouveau) hippies, college English or history majors, itinerant actors and artists in search of commercial freedom. Some percentage of each category gets lost in the fantasy of the faire way of life and never really gets out. The allure of this fringe existence is considerable, with a traveling, extended family living a fairy tale existence as knights and damsels ten hours a day. Add in the gypsy encampment life at night that confirms the "specialness" performers feel and the apartness that can be so lonely unless a peer group shares it. It is a living *Dungeons & Dragons* game that can be a hard drug to kick.

In my case, an ex-wife whom I met, married and divorced in three successive years of Renaissance faires kicked me off the habit. Well, mostly. I was back at the Great Eastern Ren Faire, the GERF. I had a monkey on my back, and it wore tights and a doublet.

Great Eastern had only hired a skeleton crew to do a tilt exhibition—where the riders do a series of mounted games—and a ground fight to promote the GERF, which was three months later.

The Cloisters Faire was free to the public as compared to the overpriced for-profit faire, but it brought the GERF a lot of customers and so wasn't considered "competition."

We pro-rennies were determined to give the public more than its money's worth. The producers, Dawn and Barry, thought they owned the concept of the Renaissance and so made a point of homing in on any event even vaguely pre-twentieth century. I had no reason to complain because hey, I was working, and they were paying me.

The area of the festival swelled out from the loop walk around the Cloisters down to the meadow below where the tilt field was set, extending along the half mile or so tarmac road all the way to the main gate of the parkland by the Botanical Gardens. The roadway was lined with merchants setting up temporary booths and folding tables barely disguised as period for the entire length of the road. It ran in a spiral that led up to the Cloisters itself. All the way up I saw lots of familiar faces with many people waving and collected a few hugs along the way.

At ten o'clock on that Sunday, I found myself helping fellow Silver Swan members Neville St. Cloud and Robin Madden set up their PVC and cloth booth partway up.

"Geez, guys," I complained as I held an upright pipe for Robin to screw in a crosspiece, "were one of you ladies frightened by Lincoln logs as a child?"

"Quiet, Atlas," Robin said, "I can't screw with all that noise."

"Oh really," Neville snickered, "I didn't think your hearing was connected there."

Robin paused for a second, then realized what she had said and turned beet red (which went from hair root to ample bosom) and faked a coughing fit.

"You're just too easy a target," Neville said to Robin. "I don't get any points at all for making you blush." Neville St. Cloud was black-haired, rail thin, pale as a Welsh ghost with violet eyes that smiled all the time. She was an editor at a children's book publisher and a founding member of the Silver Swan group.

Neville and Robin sold mostly Mandy Seaton's soft sculpture heads but had supplemented their selling stock with some costume items, plastic swords for kids and a couple of tankards, sword hangers and some nice wool cloaks.

Mandy herself couldn't be there because of some Midwest family issue, but the Silver Swan booth was always manned at events by a revolving roster of the members (including myself occasionally).

"I just saw the horse trailer pull down the road," Neville said. "You should get your rehearsal in. We'll finish up here."

I made the last connection on the overhead PVC and stepped down to put on my chainmail shirt again.

Chainmail, for those who've never seen a crusader movie, is interlocked metal rings that when made right, are capable of turning most sword blows. It was all the rage from the eleven hundreds on, worn even under the heavy plate armor of what most think of as the traditional knight.

Most Hollywood versions are woven rope sprayed silver, or aluminum links because the eighteen gauge steel links are heavy. My "vest," a six-in-one weave, was actually supposed to be able to stop a forty-five-caliber handgun.

"I tested it on a watermelon," said the guy who sold it to me. "Pulped the melon, but the bullet never got through the weave." I have never had any interest in proving him a liar.

I had the vest made when I'd done some bodyguard/door security work some years before. I seldom wore it at faires, even though it was a real attention getter and made me look like robo-bad guy because it weighed forty damn pounds.

All that weight was on my shoulders and tightly cinched belt at my waist, which also meant a heavy padded jacket under the vest to keep my delicate skin unchafed. Wearing it in the summer season was insane, and my opinion of crusaders who wore that stuff in Middle Eastern heat veered between respect and disbelief.

I had decided to challenge myself since it was a cool June, under the excuse that I needed to get in shape for the season. In fact, I let vanity instead of sanity rule and wore the darn thing 'cause it looked cool.

I was all suited up, coif on my head, and was belting on my sword when a bubbly little voice behind me squealed, "Mommy."

A tiny blur raced past me into Robin's arms. Little Danny had his mother's dark coloring and his father's Nordic features. Big Dan followed his five-year-old with a stiff-legged walk that said he was already pissed off with the day.

"Well, hello, Dan," I offered. I towered over him and must have looked like Ironman.

He stared daggers at me and nodded. "Eric."

"Hello, baby," Robin gushed, pulling little Danny into a hug. "Mommy didn't expect to see you until much later." She shot an accusing look at Dan.

"'Prize you! 'prize you," Danny happily exclaimed.

"He got all antsy about seeing you at breakfast," Dan said. "I was gonna take him to the park anyway, so I figured he could stop by now. I'll take him around here and the little park down by the A train at Two Hundred Street."

He looked straight at Robin for reproach. We all knew she was having a hard time not being with Dan and had hoped to focus on the busy day ahead.

Dan was supposed to deliver their son near closing and quickly depart. Now we all knew he would end up hanging out at the booth half the day, giving Robin no mental space. Robin knew it too, but to her credit she managed a crisp "How nice" at Dan and went back to hugging the tyke.

"I gotta get to rehearsal," I threw into the mix. "I'll catch you guys later." Then as an afterthought I said, "Bring Danny by after the lunch tilt and I'll give him the 'Lone Ranger' special ride."

Dan looked like he wanted to object on general principles, but Danny burst out with "Hi Yo Silver! Hi Yo Silver!" and it shut Pop up. I just smiled.

I can be such a bitch!

Smitty and Vita were waiting for me when I got back to the improvised barrier of trash bins and police barricades that we laughingly referred to as "the corral." Both were suited up for the day and ready to rehearse.

"Hey guys," I said giving Vita a hug. "Ready to get this cluster flick up and running?"

"Have been for an hour," Vita said. "What kept you? Did ya have trouble getting out of bed without a crane?"

I high-fived Smitty before I answered.

"The Swedish stewardesses wouldn't let me leave until they were all tired." I snickered.

Vita laughed, and Smitty blushed a deep crimson.

Smitty had been my assistant for nearly a year. At five ten, and one hundred and thirty pounds of German-Irish Boy Scout, with enthusiasm and honesty to match, he was a great fight captain and aide. He was also a juggler, leather worker, stage fighter, and ex-student of mine—and a pleasure to be around.

"Just one little problem," I said, looking around. "Did anyone see a cowboy and some horses?" The "corral" was painfully empty.

"Kelly and Carlos took them for a walk," Vita said. "They were real nervous after the trailer ride."

Kelly was in charge of the horses and rode opposite me in the joust the last two years at the faire. He affected a long handlebar mustache that, with his long sandy hair, made him look like he should be riding with the Dalton Gang. I think he would have liked that too. He rode like a centaur, drank like a fish and had the morals of a teenage rabbit, but he was always on the mark in joust or ground fight and was as even-keeled as a canal barge.

Carlos, along with Smitty, worked the stable where we kept the faire's joust horses. He had come along to handle the nags that the cheapo producers had rented for us to use for our tilt. It takes months to train two horses to run at each other and not freak out. The two trained ones that had been used for the past three years were in their winter home in southern Pennsylvania and not scheduled up until early July. So we had decided not to do a full-out joust and were doing a "sporting tilt" instead.

"Might as well work on our part of the ground fight 'til the nags arrive," I suggested.

"How about you win this time," Vita offered, "just to freak out the civilians?" Vita was in her mid-twenties. She and I had dated briefly when we first met, but she had quickly become my "little sister" and resident pain in the butt for three years both in and out of my stage combat classes. She was lithe and blonde with her features fixed in a perpetual smirk.

"You know damn well if I pretend to kill you, the audience will really lynch me!" I said with emphasis. No joke.

Once for "grins" we changed the end of a fight, so Vita ended up dead. The crowd got so ugly, so quickly that we improvised a new ending on the spot with her having only "played possum." I then promptly lost. Moral: the big guy better lose to the pretty Lithuanian for the family to have a feel-good day!

"Then defend yourself, you son of a pig!" she said and launched herself in slow motion at my eyes, claws extended. I caught her hands, and we slow-motioned through the unarmed portion of the fight we would do at the final tilt.

We had already decided on the phone to cannibalize two fights we had done before: the sword fight we had done last summer (and at two corporate events some months back) and the unarmed fight I had choreographed for a *Taming of the Shrew* back in April, on which she had assisted me.

Smitty and Kelly were doing a much shorter fight since Smitty (as my evil sidekick) blindsided Kelly with a breakaway lance after he had unseated me. I am then about to do him in when Vita intervenes and we go at it.

It had to be a very clear good vs. evil scenario for the story to play to the back row and short enough that we could rehearse it the "morning of." We wanted everyone—including us—to have a good experience so safety was first on the plate. There was enough pageantry to please the crowd without us smacking each other for real.

Eventually Kelly and Carlos came back with the horses. The mounts were standard-bred horses and had enough pep to do what we need. Kelly had spent the day before working them so he knew they would be up to the show.

We plugged Kelly into the fight in a couple of minutes and then he and I "walked" the tilt routine on foot in the space we would be working in. Then we did a quick ride though, mocking the actions. My mount was a little skittish but he would do.

The morning parade was at eleven. The actors, led by us, ushered the public in, made a circuit of the joust field and then the faire was on. Went back to rehearse the ground fight a couple of more times and then rested for the first show.

For the lunchtime "tilt" we rode at bales of hay and speared them, rode at melons on poles and sliced them up with straight Patton cavalry sabers (non-period, but hey, it's a show), and then argued over the score and got into a shouting match that resulted in a "challenge-to-joust" for the five o'clock show. It was great hokum and we all felt good about it.

Unfortunately, after I picketed the horses and made my way to the Swan booth to get lunch, I ran into another shouting match. This time it was a real one between Dan Madden and Tom De Dannin.

"I don't need some gigolo Mick tellin' me how to discipline my son!" Dan was in a full-bore snit, held back by Neville, while little Danny cried against Robin's shoulder.

Tom stood stark still, Jillian off to his left with one pale hand resting on his left shoulder. I knew that meant she was clearing his way to fight and from the grinning sneer on his face I knew he was more than ready.

His street name had been Grinner and nobody in their right mind wanted to fight him when he had that look on.

Time for me to play peacemaker.

I sauntered my mail-clad two meters right up to big Dan—a relative term since he came barely to my shoulder—eased Neville aside and clamped my hand on his shoulder. "Hey, Dan," I said in as innocent a voice as I could muster. "How's your day goin'?"

Jillian took the hint and pulled Tom away from the gathering crowd. Neville went along to help calm little Danny.

"Let go of me, you big freak," Dan said in a really endearing tone. "That Irish shit has no right telling me how to raise my son!"

Neville was back at my left ear now. "He slapped Danny's butt pretty hard for running into the crowd. Tom told him to take it easy, and Mr. Calm here flew off the handle."

Dan tried to squirm out of my pseudo-Vulcan nerve pinch, but I was having none of it.

"He has no right—" he began.

"Can it," I injected. "Everybody has an opinion, Dan. You have to let it roll off you like water off a duck."

"Don't you start tellin' me my business," Danny said.

"If it happens here, it is my business." It's amazing how fast bouncer-speak asserts itself. I gave him my coldest stare and warmest smile—a winning combination with the drunk set in the East Village bar I used to do security at.

Dan looked venomously at me. "There will be a reckoning. You and Tom better keep a look over your shoulders from now on." He shot a hard look at Robin.

"The kid's yours 'til next week." He turned and left.

Tom joined me, his grin now a relaxed one. "I wonder if he gives A-hole lessons?" he said. "He must have a PhD in it."

––––––––––

The rest of the afternoon was a little more relaxed and the five o'clock fight went off by the numbers. I lost heroically (or villainously, depending on your POV) and the crowd dispersed as it got dark.

Despite his dad's blow up, the rest of Danny's day was a good one. He yelled "Hi Yo Silver" as I rode him in circles around the tilting field on the jousting horse. He got a little wooden sword and shield and showed me just how King Arthur did in Godzilla (he was at the mix-and-match story stage).

The Swan booth made some money, and we all had fun running around in tights. Tom dropped his bombshell of the day on me as we were packing up the gear to go home: "Tommy Gunns called me back before we left the house. He's arranged a lunch meeting tomorrow!" He hesitated only a moment before adding, "I want you to shadow us and watch my back."

He gave me no chance to react. He turned with an arm around Jillian and said over his shoulder, "Talk to you tomorrow about it; see you about one." And he was gone.

Smitty went with Kelly and the horses. I threw a trench coat over my chain vest and with Vita's help, we carried two duffel bags full of swords and gear downhill to Two Hundredth Street and the A Train.

"I'm hungry," Vita panted when we hit the bottom of the stairs. "Let's get something." She lived out in Queens as well but off the number seven line. It was a long ride and a two-train switch.

"I'll buy," I said magnanimously, "as long as it's cheap. Let's do deli."

We entered the corner bodega at Two Hundredth. Vita greeted the old Korean man behind the counter in his language.

We had been inside barely two minutes when three punks burst into the store and pistol-whipped the Korean shopkeeper. Then they ran through the store grabbing items that caught their fancy. They also did their best to terrorize the owner's teenage daughter, Vita and myself with animal-like growls and curses to prove how tough they were.

One of the thugs shoved a cheap handgun in my face. I felt as if I were in a bad monogram spy movie. Never having been faced with a situation like that before, I had a dearth of clever ideas.

The punks looked as if they weren't going to leave until they really hurt someone. As the largest white guy in the store, I was likely on their "hurt somebody list," so I fell back on an old reliable answer to senseless violence: more senseless violence.

I hauled off and "slapped" Vita across her pretty face. "Stupid Cow!" I yelled. "If you didn't insist on condoms we wouldn't be in here!"

The boy with the gun didn't think it was funny, but the other two hoods started to giggle. Vita teared at the eyes, nodded her head imperceptibly and screamed, "Defend yourself, you son of a pig!" as she went for my eyes with her long fingernails in pure wench fashion. I caught her wrists and we struggled.

That did it for Gunboy, who laughed like a jackass with asthma. He was tall and skinny with a shaven, round head. That combined with bad acne made him look truly moonfaced. I guess we must have looked funny—me with the old trench coat making me look even larger than usual, and Vita's slim five foot four. With her long blonde hair, apple-sized breasts, and dressed as a medieval wench—which meant Wonderbra provided cleavage—it must have looked more like she was trying to scale me rather than fight me. A real crowd-pleaser.

"Hey, Angelo!" The squat black punk who was playing with a kitchen knife laughed at our struggles. "If he can't control his woman, maybe we can."

"Nobody can control a woman with that look on her face," Moonfaced Angelo wheezed. He was rooting through the cash register as he spoke. The injured Korean owner lay bleeding near his feet. The man's daughter was sobbing as she tried to stanch the blood flowing from her father's head.

Vita all but foamed at the mouth as she yelled every invective she knew (some I hadn't even heard before) and apparently still trying like blazes to claw my eyes out. Hidden in those snarls were Korean words to the daughter, "Stay down and cover him!" and to me, "Go for Moonface."

I let her pull a hand free and do the fake eye-rake. She swiped across my eyes so fast that no one could see that it was the fingerpads and not the nails that made contact. I screamed in pain, called her a "puta" for the benefit of Moonface who laughed harder and angled himself for a better view of what was to come next.

With my butt toward Moonface, I was doubled over with my knees bent for a powerful spring. I covered my face to hide the fact that there was no blood from the nails.

Vita and I had worked together so long that we were practically telepathic in improvisational acting situations and staged fights. She threw her stage right cross close enough to my face that I felt the wind.

I hid the sound-effects snap and snapped my head around with close-up realism. It rocked me back to within two feet of the counter.

Moonfaced Angelo was laughing and wheezing and trying to yell to us to stop at the same time. "Halto!" He motioned to the third member of the gang with his gun. "Grab her!" he managed to squeeze out.

The third musketeer was a white kid with a shaven head whose face resembled a map of Ireland. He was a weightlifter and had that monkey-man hunch to his shoulders that made you wonder if he had a neck under the bomber jacket. He made a grab for Vita, who slipped him. She grabbed a bottle of ketchup off the shelf and lobbed it at me. I dodged. It sailed past me at shoulder height and almost hit Angelo, who flinched and instinctively angled his body to avoid the missile.

That was it!

I stepped on a milk crate that held bags of rice and launched myself over the crowded counter. I slammed into Moonface's right shoulder, pinning the gun arm to him and slammed both of us into and through the plate glass window of the store.

This was not as nuts as it sounded. I buried my head in his shoulder, kept my hands down behind his body mass, and I had an ace to play: the chainmail shirt!

So when I hit Angelo, I was something like a three-hundred-pound cannonball that carried Moonface and me a good six feet out onto the sidewalk where I landed on him with a crunch sound from his ribs.

I shoulder-rolled off my Hispanic crash pad Angelo, shucked my trench coat, and was back into the bodega door before the glass finished falling from the frame.

While Muscles was watching me play Peter Pan, Vita had blindsided him with a second ketchup bottle. He fell, sprawled over a potato chip rack—a mass of tomato, hemoglobin and glass shards. The black punk backed Vita down one of the aisles with that mean-looking kitchen knife. She didn't dare try to block it and couldn't risk turning to run, so she kept inching down the aisle and chucked corn flake and Bisquick boxes at him. He was not amused, but bless her Lithuanian heart, the expression on her face was not fear so much as annoyance.

I didn't relish getting in close to that knife, but I had stupidly left the pistol tangled in the coat I'd left on the sidewalk.

It might as well have been on Mars, because I didn't dare leave her alone. I looked around frantically for something to bean him with, and my eyes lit on our duffel bag of gear. I ran to it, tore the zipper down and pulled out my one-handed Viking sword and a round wooden shield. I faced the aisle and cried at the top of my lungs, "Odin!"

The black tough guy turned, got one look at me backlit by the orange evening sunlight and his eyes bugged out. I'm sure with my long hair disheveled and with the four-foot blade in my hand I looked like Armageddon straight on. His eyes rolled back in his head and dropped like a bad lawsuit.

He actually fainted dead away like a character out of a Tex Avery cartoon.

After that it was all quick and by the book—911, paperwork and the inevitable, "I'll sue your ass off!" from the newly awakened tough guy.

Muscles and Moonface were still out cold when they loaded them into the ambulance. One of the cops wanted to book me for possession of a concealed weapon, but his sergeant had done security at the medieval faire and had seen my day act, and I had my union cards with me. So, although they impounded them for evidence, I was pretty sure I'd get them back through channels.

It was almost nine o'clock before we climbed on the train. Adrenaline fatigue kept us silent the whole trip. When it came time for Vita to get off at Queensborough Plaza to transfer to the Number Seven, she smiled up at me with that evil grin of hers. "My idea to get condoms?"

I tried to look nonplussed. "It was the only thing that came to mind at the time. After all, you can't be too careful?" I ducked as she swung. She dashed for the exit; the train doors closed behind her.

I do live a charmed life.

Chapter Four

Rehearsal for a Renaissance faire is pretty much like rehearsal for any other show, except for the sheer numbers involved. The Faire employed close to two hundred performers back then (recessions hit even that business), most as "environmental performers." That translates to walking set decorations that interact with the patrons on the ten-acre grounds. They give the place the atmosphere of an old English village faire like a giant interactive CD or *Dungeons & Dragons* game.

My concern as fight master was with the members of what we called "the Fight Corps." They consisted of seventeen actors hired primarily because they had some physical skill. They would be the King's Guards, Highwaymen band members, knights and villagers, who would fight in a living chess game, highwayman scenes, the joust melee and a few assorted court and villager scenes that had scripted fights. A Ren faire makes much of pageant and action to fill the outdoor venue.

"Okay, folks," I said to this, the first assembly of my corps (most of them anyway; a small number had previous commitments). "While all of us who work the faire hope our acting counts, most of us in the fight corps know we were hired sight unseen."

There rose a general titter and hubbub at that. Most had signed on for weekends in the country and proximity to New York, not to stretch their acting muscles. I held up my hands in a calculatedly theatrical gesture.

"We also know that acting is seventy-five percent of staged combat; the rest is pure technique. No matter how lazy you are as actors this summer," I concluded, "You will be dead-on with that technique. This summer, zero injuries! I, your emperor, have spoken."

This time it was a chorus of "Oh yes, oh mighty one" from the Ren faire veterans, most of whom bowed prostrate. The neophytes just stared in amazement.

The other difference in my part of Ren faire work from the acting or dance troupes is the close ties it fosters. In an acting scene, if you blow a line you just annoy your fellow actors. In a choreographed fight scene, if you screw up you can kill somebody.

All of us who had previously worked together knew and trusted each other's abilities and limitations on and off the Faire grounds. Facing ten thousand patrons a day in improvised acting scenes fosters an "us against them, we've been in the trenches" esprit de corps.

The Ren faire producers had brilliantly bought a loft and office floor in Chelsea to save costs on fight and dance rehearsals, never once thinking we might need more than an eight-foot ceiling or a decent suspended floor (instead of tile over concrete). Naturally the dance choreographer and I insisted on other spaces.

Dawn and Barry agreed but tried to nickel and dime us more than usual. The rehearsal space we were using that year was on Thirteenth Street, between Sixth and Fifth Avenues, down the block and across the street from the Quad Cinema and my old alma mater, Parsons School of Design. It was a first-floor loft/theater space with four annoyingly placed central columns in an otherwise great sprung wood floor. It had eighteen-foot ceilings and no hanging lights to snag unwary quarterstaves. The space was a fight choreographer's dream!

"Want me to get 'em warmed up, Chief?" Smitty asked. Talk about a "gosh wow!" attitude.

"Naw." I smiled. "I'll run 'em into the ground myself." I motioned everyone to their feet. "Let's run!" I did a couple of easy jogs around the room as everyone fell in behind me and then picked up the pace. A few grapevine steps followed. After running backwards, we stretched. I use stretches from dance, yoga, Aikido and a number of other sources since staged combat is the hybrid child of martial and theatrical arts.

"I can only get in that position when I'm in love," Vita said as we did downward-facing dog. "Otherwise, it hurts too much."

I looked up from the wide "V" of my open legs as I rolled back into a split and grinned fiendishly. Then I said in my best Peter Lorre voice: "Then learn to love the pain." A chorus of groans erupted all round.

After warm-ups we did some basic rapier cut drills. I run basics at the beginning of every rehearsal period to make sure everyone had the same choreographic vocabulary. Even though Vita, Smitty and a few others had either worked or taken class together, I broke down the parries, cuts and basic footwork.

A half hour of that got everybody up to speed and in sync. I made sure they all moved around to work with different partners.

Like dancing, stunt combat is as much a matter of partnering as individual skill. After the first session, I would huddle with Smitty and Vita to get their take on everybody and start working the actual pairs who would fight at the faire by the next week.

About eleven o'clock I gave everyone a short break, endured a bit of ribbing about Vita and my adventure at the Cloisters (which had made the *Post* "Robin Hood of Inwood") and then excused myself to use the phone in the office to call my answering service.

I was hoping for a call from Jimmy, the casting director at Guiding Light. I hadn't worked for him in almost a month, and I was about due. I dress up well with my long hair pinned up as fourth cop from the left in the police station scenes. No luck. I only had a message from Tom De Dannin that everything was still on schedule.

Man, was I nervous.

I went back and finished the rehearsal with my mind only half there. I said nothing to Smitty or Vita.

After we put the practice weapons away I congratulated everybody on a good first day.

I wanted to scream, "Look at me I'm having an adventure!" but showed admirable restraint with a "See ya tomorrow!"

One fifteen found me lurking in one of those instant porn video stores that pop up for a few months or so then vanish only to reappear in another part of the city. This one happened to be located across the street from the printing house where Tom worked.

I wandered around the European bondage video section, which afforded a full view of the front entrance to Tom's building. I'd been there, duffel bag slung over my shoulder, for ten minutes, trying hard to decide amongst the catholic forms of politically incorrect sex tapes. Actually, I was trying hard to look like I was going to buy something so the Pakistani store manager wouldn't make noise at me.

I was truly developing an appreciation for the varied uses for latex when I saw Tom exit his building. I hung back a few moments. Since I knew where Tom was headed, as well as his route, there was no real need to stay close to him. My job was to cover his back in case there were any new developments. I watched as he walked down the street at a casual pace, scanning the crowd behind him to see if there were any new players in the game.

There was one.

I spotted the new face walking with apparent casualness a block behind Tom, on the opposite side of the street from him.

The guy was good, pausing to look in a card shop window or at a posted handbill on a lamp post, but his manner was too relaxed for someone moving at the pace Tom's lanky stride had set. Each time he stopped his window shopping, his sunglasses zeroed in on Tom the block or two ahead before reassuming a mask of casual tourism.

Tom and I had plotted a zig-zag path down Varick to West Broadway and on to Canal Street with a couple of doglegs to be sure. The tail was a tad under six feet and rangy. He moved like an antelope that had been forced to wear ankle weights, with a loose and bouncy walk that he tried to hide. His movement quality would have made him stand out even if he hadn't also had long sandy-blond hair and a GQ model's face.

He'd tried to dress down to the neighborhood with a worn old denim long coat, embroidered with patches along the left sleeve and down the front left side. I wasn't close enough to see for sure, but they looked like patches from different countries.

He wore a Rolex watch on his right wrist that he glanced at from time to time, and the pants and shoes that showed beneath the coat looked expensive. Then again, considering that my black New Balance referee shoes were held together with black gaffer's tape, almost anything looked expensive to me.

The Double Eagle was a Tex-Mex chili place on the northeast corner of Canal and West Broadway, opposite a row of hole-in-the-wall discount electronic places. Tom went in and sat at a booth by himself.

"Blondie" settled into a clothing store down the block on the south side of Canal. I picked an electronics graveyard that had a sign proclaiming "Yankee Trader Audio Parts" on the southwest corner of Canal, where I could watch both Tom and Blondie.

About five minutes later a dark-haired man in a bomber jacket walking east along Canal Street went into the restaurant. He went straight to Tom's booth, greeted him and sat down.

The plot thickens; the Marshal meets Mr. Gunns Cavendish at the saloon while faithful Festus keeps an eye on Doc Holliday.

I laughed aloud, standing there in the store. *What a shamus I make.* There I stood, my old NATO-issue surplus blue trench coat belted tight about me, a shoulder bag and an army surplus duffel with two epees in it slung over my shoulder, all inconspicuous six foot six of me.

I remember someone, I think Salvador Dali, saying that "If you want to be noticed, wax your mustache and wear a cape—unless you are in New York, where no one will notice." I laughed again and then got a grip before somebody noticed I was auditioning for the funny farm and settled in to watch.

The half hour went by slowly, with me working to keep myself focused on watching Tom, Mr. Gunns and Blondie. A lot of attractive, artsy-type young women wandered in and out of Pearl Paints Art Supply up the block. Many attractive Asian young women walked to and fro, reminding me that Chinatown was half a dozen blocks east.

The rumbling in my stomach reminded me of how good Chinese food would be and how hungry I was. Visions of chicken fried rice began to dance in my head.

Tom and Mr. Gunns stood up, shook hands and parted. Tom went back west along Canal Street with no sign he expected to see me. Mr.

Gunns watched him go, boring holes into Tom's back with a steady gaze for a full minute. Then he turned, with no notice of Blondie and headed east on Canal.

I watched Blondie. Mr. Gunns was important but now that Blondie was on the scene, it was a Lady or the Tiger choice. If Blondie followed Tom, I'd follow Mr. Gunns. If not, I'd watch the watchdog as long as I could.

My stomach was screaming for food. I was considering ditching the whole thing when Blondie started walking west along Canal. He passed right in front of the store I was in, and I got a closer look at him.

I had been right. The patches on the coat were from different countries, and there were pins of all sorts too—Montreal, Hamburg, Detroit, were a few I could read. He was as *GQ* close up as he had been at a distance but with a London West End spin. I didn't get a clear look at his face because he had big sunglasses and long bangs that hid most of his features, but his left ear was triple pierced with little gold hoops, as if Mick Jagger wanted to be Errol Flynn. Most of his expression behind the hair and glasses was a mystery.

His brisk pace copied Tom's, and he was gone quickly. I was out of the store, headed East, and going double time to catch up with Mr. Gunns. He was two blocks ahead of me on the north side of Canal Street between Greene and Broadway, headed straight into Chinatown.

His bomber jacket was relatively easy to spot in the crowd, though I was fortunate he hadn't turned off onto a side Street. He moved through the heart of Chinatown with his pace an easy, confident one. It made me think he had a definite destination. He moved along following Canal all the way to Bowery at the foot of the Manhattan Bridge.

He definitely was going somewhere, though in no great hurry. He crossed Bowery near the Rosemary Theater and went beside the bridge.

I followed like Lamont Cranston, unseen and unheard but looking for the evil in the heart of men.

School kids played in the schoolyard at Chrystie Street, most of them Asian. I saw a Latina policewoman, looking like a miniature statue, watching the playground and the street.

I had an almost overwhelming urge to run up to her and yell, "Hey, Officer, I'm following this bad guy gun dealer, cool, huh?" but restrained myself.

Mr. Tommy Gunns continued on and passed the Sun Sing Theater, a Chinese-language movie theater actually housed in the arch of one of the bridge supports. Tom, A.C., and I had all spent a good many of our collective Saturday nights there watching kick-and-scream films. I made a mental note to check what movie was playing on the way back.

Mr. Gunns went two blocks farther south, rounded a corner of the Golden Hen Noodle Shop and went down an alley. It was "Something" Place, but the street sign had been defaced with paint.

I lagged back as much as I dared, but with the blocks being so short, I feared losing him. When I rounded the corner of the alley only two minutes behind him, I found myself alone in a classic blind alley.

It was straight out of a comic book—thirty feet long, and with white steam from a drycleaners billowing out to creep along the cobblestones.

"Sucker!" I whispered through clenched teeth. "It was a set up." There were three doors he could have gone in.

I tried all three; all of them were locked.

I circled the block twice, hoping he had just ducked into the building as part of an established pattern to throw off a tail.

I hung around watching the alley for an hour, but Mr. Gunns didn't come out.

I finally left, discouraged and feeling very tall and white in that neighborhood.

Both pictures at the Sun Sing I'd seen already and hadn't liked. Both were bloody gang pictures where there were no clear-cut good guys and everybody dies.

Some Lamont Cranston I turned out to be; great adventure? Hah.!

Where's the Hardy Boys when you need them?

Chapter Five

A week after my terrible failure, on a Monday morning, I was in Tom and Jill's living room. I'd come to mind the apartment while they went into court.

"I feel like such a dork," I said to Jillian. "I lost the only other Caucasian in a ten-block radius."

"Could be that's how he spotted you," she tried to console me.

Jill was finally sorting bills for the housing court appeal. She was always sorting something, a valiant but futile effort against the enfolding entropy of their lives.

"You're just a tall geek," Tom said charitably. "He would have spotted you in Glasgow."

"You're so understanding." Jill threw him a glance that could freeze hydrogen.

"Oh, it's all right, I deserve that."

I really felt like an A-1 class screw up for losing Mr. Gunns. Even a good rehearsal week hadn't shaken me of that feeling.

"Oh, lighten up, man," Tom said. "Anybody would have lost the guy in a set up like that, even the terror of Baltimore's crime lords." When he saw the puzzled look on my face he added, "He probably didn't spot you. Why would he even look?"

"You mean it?"

"You can be a real putz, man. Of course I mean it. Either that's where he was going in the first place, or it was SOP after a meet in case of a tail. Don't sweat it."

"Of course he means it," Jill said with false sincerity, batting her eyes at Tom. "After his confession to me this week, he wouldn't dare tell an untruth ever again, right, hon?"

Tom grimaced and picked up a pile of old Silver Swan Newsletters and SF magazines that she had bundled for recycling.

"I'll go see if José has heard anything on the landlord's plans," Tom said. He touched the pin on his beret in salute, winked at me and headed out the door.

"He's entitled to rib me. After all, he did call me in on that little adventure. It was fun."

She sorted bills with furious intensity. After a time she looked up. "I don't like the whole thing, Eric. I just wish he'd let it drop."

"I think it's done and over with anyway," I said with not a little disappointment in my voice. "If I was spotted they'll think their cover was blown, and from what Tom said the guy was really antsy at the meeting anyway."

"I hope you're right," she said. "Tom has an odd way of finding crusades in every challenge. The romantic in him, I suppose. It's why I can't even be as angry with him about the gambling as I should be."

"Yeah. After he told me I was just a little afraid you might have busted his skull on general principles."

"We had a pretty huge fight over it," she admitted. "But it's that child part of him I love as much as I hate. I think that's the definition of a romantic."

"Like you're not, Oh Daughter of Ireland?"

Jill threw a paperback novel at me and pouted. "I'm serious," she insisted. "He should know better after his time in the gangs. He really does romanticize the world too much. Of course, when it comes to the important things, he's Mr. Blasé. You know how he proposed to me?" She stood with fists on hips. "He was soaking in the bathtub. I was sprawled on the bed—completely exhausted after another convention. He murmurs, 'Why don't we get married at the World Fantasy Con?'"

Jill smiled, her face suddenly gone from soft as she relished the memory. "To this day, I don't know if I accepted because I wanted to marry him or because I was too tired to say no."

I laughed out loud. "With the breath reserves you have, Jill, you definitely didn't surrender out of exhaustion!" She chucked another book at me, and I dodged. We both laughed. Then she glanced at the clock.

"He thinks he's being a real smart guy," Jill said. "His idea is to bullshit with José long enough that I'll go without him."

"I'll go up and get him, hon."

"Good," she said. "I'll finish getting these together. Even if we are thinking of moving, I don't want it to be over this. That landlord owes us." She dove back into the pile of bills.

I climbed the stairs to José's office, but he hadn't seen Tom. Weird.

I hurried down from the super's apartment and told Jillian that Tom hadn't been up there. She cursed, the corners of her mouth turned down. "Damn that Mick husband of mine. He's taken off to a bar. Court was too much for him." She made a strangling gesture with her hands.

"I'll go get him."

"Thanks, Eric. It's either the Silver Swan or O'Leary's. You know where they are!"

I nodded and was out the door, leaving Jillian sorting bills and cursing Irish husbands.

I had to laugh. *Tom, you're a putz to piss her off again.* My real sympathies were for anyone who crossed Jill in court that afternoon.

It made sense, Tom's nerve breaking about the court appearance. His only brushes with the law had all been during his gang days and as a result of his and Jillian's activism for Northern Ireland.

Tom had experienced another aborted adventure during that week—an attempted second meeting with Mr. Tommy Gunns to see the merchandise. It hadn't worked out any better than the first.

As Tom put it, "I sat in a bar 'til twelve o'clock on a work night while two of New York's finest and some jerk from the ATF drank beers at the taxpayers' expense. Tommy Boy never showed." It helped me feel like less of a fool and gave me hope that the whole thing was done and over.

When I got downstairs to the lobby door—an old wrought iron and glass monster that weighed a ton—I saw a skinny little girl, about six years old, in a pink sweat suit trying to push it open.

"I got it, honey," I said and almost pulled her off her feet when it swung out.

"Thank you, Mister," she called over her shoulder as she raced away.

Aha, I thought, *civilization has at least one generation more to go.* I watched her as she ran to an excited little playmate who pointed around the building, and then the two of them flew off around the corner into the service alley. I turned the other way, walked to the corner and crossed the street as I headed for the Swan, which was the closer of the two bars Jillian had suggested.

That's when I saw the ambulance.

It was coming down Thirty-Sixth Street from Bay Ridge Avenue. I don't know why I felt it, but the moment I saw the ambulance speed past me and around the corner of Thirty-Sixth, I felt as if a cold hand had grabbed my heart.

I was running past the building before I even realized it, dodging the group of people who swarmed out from the front door and racing down the service alley.

A crowd had already gathered at the end of the alley where it opened onto the concrete courtyard behind the building. I pushed my way through the crowd, holding my breath, not daring to breathe. When I saw the blue uniformed cop, I knew my worst fear was true.

I knew what I would see before I even looked at the body of what had been my best friend.

Tom lay on his back in the center of the courtyard, his right leg crossed under the left and slightly bent. His arms were thrown open wide, palms up as if some sort of perverted crucifixion image and his handsome black-Irish face was fixed in one last mischievous, challenging grin.

He still wore that stupid, plain black beret. Only now, those blue eyes were forever open and empty. A dark stain oozed out from under the beret.

I must have said something classic, like "Oh my God," or "Oh Tom," because one of the two cops turned from writing in his notebook to look at me.

"Did you know him?" the officer asked. He didn't sound as if he was all that interested in what I did or didn't know.

I turned away and found myself staring into the face of the little girl from the door. There was a jelly stain around her mouth I hadn't noticed before. She had pretty blue eyes that were so full of life and they were focused through the legs of the crowd to try and see what was going on.

"Sir," the cop asked again, "Did you know him?" Did … past tense.

"Yes. Apartment 2B. Tom De Dannin."

I turned before he could question me further and ran back up the alley. I ran past the empty gurney being brought from the ambulance. I ran back through the heavy door, back up the chipped marble stairs three at a time and through the door marked 2B.

A smiling Jillian stood looking at the neatly stacked pile of bills when I flung the door open. She looked up and into my eyes and all the color drained from her face.

I don't know how she knew, whether some expression on my face, posture of my body, or the cold darkness I felt in my soul escaped through my eyes, but with a hideous certainty, she knew.

"Oh my God, Tom's dead!" She took a half step forward, scattering the stacks of bills and swayed like a drunk.

I moved to catch her, but she waved me off. She mouthed the word "how" but no sound came out.

"A fall, I think. I …" The words were so meaningless. "The police are there," I added.

She stared at me, her green eyes wide and misting. Not crying yet; the reality of the pain was just distant enough to hold back the tears.

The clock in the living room that Tom had made by gutting a Smurf doll and sticking an alarm clock in its belly showed 10:21 a.m. Its ticks seemed as loud as Big Ben.

Corwin the Cat sauntered into the room, looked at the two of us and turned with disdain toward another room.

Jill looked so much like a librarian, dressed as she was for court in a grey skirt suit, blue blouse and heels. She wore a little silver and topaz swan pin that our group gave her last Christmas for editing our newsletter. Somewhere on the street a dog barked like a cannon going off.

"There are police!" she said in a firm voice. "You have to get rid of the pot." I stared back at her for a moment, not quite believing what she was saying. "There's a bong on the nightstand and a stash in the drawer. You have to get rid of them!" She was quite serious about it. A lifetime as a respectable teacher and student activist cut through even the shock and had her defaulting to "cover up" mode.

"I'm going to make some tea," she announced in a calm, almost toneless voice and hurriedly walked down the hall to the kitchen. The scattered pile of bills, like so much else now, were irrelevant and forgotten.

I followed her to the kitchen.

She was, indeed, making tea. I watched her as she went through the comforting ritual of filling the kettle, placing it on the stove and pouring tea leaves from a tin into the little metal spherically shaped tea holder.

There was a desperate precision to her actions; an attention to detail that was at once horrifying and understandable. I watched her, unable to do or say anything. She was like a spring held taunt, her features rigid, her focus internal. I had no idea when she would snap or, for that matter, when it would hit me either, when the cold dead spot inside me would explode into the reality of Tom's death. It seemed to me to be some distant nightmare and was still somehow not real.

In a few minutes I saw color coming back to her cheeks, and she started to hum a tuneless melody to herself. It was like watching a marionette of the beautiful and sensitive woman I had known for so long. In some ways she seemed more lifeless than Tom had been in the alley.

A sudden explosive knock came at the door. Jillian ignored it.

Then a second knock, more insistent this time. "Police, open up." The coarse voice sounded bored.

Jillian stood still. Her expression tightened a bit, but otherwise did not change. She turned dead eyes to look at me. "I'll get the door."

I still had no words, as lost and irrational as she was in grief. I figured Jillian would be all right long enough for me to get the stash and bong from the bedroom.

The bong was on the nightstand, and the zip lock bag of marijuana was where she said it would be. The cat, Pyewacket, lay draped over the side of the dresser, looking up at me with a puzzled expression. That was nothing special, considering he was the dumbest animal I have ever known, but this time I found myself envying the cat's befuddlement. He would never miss Tom.

The bong I pocketed, and the pot I flushed.

I made it back to the entrance hall where two uniforms, a rookie and a vet, stood by the open door. Jill was talking to them calmly and civilly, asking them if they wanted tea.

"Do you know a Thomas De Dannin?" the heavyset cop asked.

"Tom is my husband," she said matter-of-factly. "His middle name is Daniel."

The two cops might as well have been asking if she had a green Chevy Nova with a broken headlight. One cop had a black notebook in hand and jotted Jillian's answers to questions about Tom.

It was all so fucking ordinary. I wanted to yell.

The kettle whistled.

Corwin made a charge at the door but turned when one of the cops shifted to look at him.

Somehow, that was the thing that made the cork pop.

Jillian screamed one long mournful, banshee wail that was too big to have come from inside her tiny body and she went for one of the cops. It was like a switch thrown: off calm, on hysteria.

I got to Jill before she got to the cop.

I scooped her up, arms pinned to her sides, while she screamed, cried, squirmed and kicked out her grief for Tom.

The kettle continued to whistle.

Jillian struggled in my arms.

Eventually, the rookie turned off the kettle. Jillian's strength gave out after a couple of minutes and she slumped in my arms, murmuring.

I set her down on the sofa. Corwin appeared on the sofa back. Jillian pulled him to her and held him. The Prince of Amber must have sensed her distress, because for once he offered no protest as she hugged and stroked him.

"And who are you?" the older cop asked me. His tone implied I was, in fact, no one and not really worth speaking to.

I studied him and blinked. He was maybe forty-five, looked a paunchy sixty and had dark Mediterranean features. He was trying to be professionally sympathetic, but he was bored with the whole process of being a cop, particularly on that day.

"A friend," I said through clenched teeth. I walked to the phone and hit the speed dial for Mandy Seaton's work number. She was a base librarian out at Fort Hamilton. Mandy and Jill talked all the time, particularly when Jill was working on a new project.

"Base Library," a male voice said.

"What's your name, friend?" the bored cop interrupted. He had his notebook and pen poised and glared at me at the edge of throwing them both down for being "challenged" by being ignored.

"Just a second, Officer," I gestured. "Mandy Seaton, please." I heard a click and a buzz while the call was transferred.

Mandy's voice answered in soft, musical tones, "Amanda Seaton speaking."

The cop was looking real pissed.

"It's Eric," I said, still not having any way to say it that wasn't brutal—I just pushed out the words: "I'm with Jillian. Tom's dead." There was a stunned silence on the other end.

"Are you at their place?" Her musical tones had dropped an octave.

"Yes. The police are here. I, uh ..."

"I'll call some people," she said. "Then I'll be over."

"Okay," I hung up.

I turned to the cop and felt a sudden surge of anger at the world. "My name is Eric Thomas Knight, with a K," I said. He wrote it down. "He was my fucking friend."

The rookie had actually poured some tea for Jillian, and she was sipping it and hugging Corwin for dear life.

"Don't give me attitude," the bored cop said in his best tough guy voice, "or I can ask these questions at the station house."

Let's hear it for the milk of human kindness.

Chapter Six

Forty-five minutes after my call to Mandy, most of the core group of the Company of the Silver Swan had either checked in to ask how they could help or to find out when and where they should show up.

The police were gone—mumbling about how "it looked like he took a dive" and with my promise to ID the body at the morgue.

Jillian had started crying again the minute the cops left, and except to walk to the door to let Lily Chan in, I sat on the sofa holding and being held by Jill. Lily let everyone else in.

Lily Chan was older than most of our group, a gaunt, short-haired blonde who'd acquired the last name by marriage. She did freelance graphics out of her apartment ten blocks from where Tom and Jillian lived. She swept in and immediately took charge of packing clothes for Jill, getting some coffee and cake and fielding any incoming calls. We artistic types let her organize any parties, showers or group trips for us. She was our ad hoc stage manager.

Robin Madden arrived by cab from Manhattan next. "I dropped off Little Danny at my father's," Robin said to Lily as she hugged her hello. Then she caught sight of Jillian and me on the sofa and hurried to where we sat.

Robin nodded to me. She sat on the other side of Jillian and quietly put her arms around her. Her tears were just as quiet.

All the features on Robin's face were individually odd, her mouth too wide, her hazel eyes a little too deep to be pretty, which was all capped by a mad mop of brunette hair. Yet somehow she radiated a beauty that melded it all together to be a stunner.

Her appeal wasn't hurt by her more than ample bosom (with her silver swan charm on a necklace flying across a field of freckled white) either. She made her living doing desktop publishing, but her heart was in fantasy writing, at which she was quite good.

We three sat in our group hug for ten minutes, wordless but eloquently lost in our commiserating grief. She grabbed hold of my shoulder and caught my eye to let me know that the loss was ours as much as Jill's.

Patrick Kelly, Neville and Don Falconson (Mandy Seaton's other half) called in during that time. They couldn't get out of work 'til five but promised to be over as soon as they could. Lily handled the calls.

I can't remember what was going through my mind during all this. Images of Tom, I guess—montage-like and disconnected. The first time I met him was at a science fiction convention. He was dressed all in black like a Brehon pirate, wearing that stupid beret with the "Free Ireland" pin. The unabashed look of joy that lit his face anytime Jillian came into the room. Himself sitting in a hotel hallway with some young kid whose girlfriend had dumped him and who'd gotten himself sick drunk. Tom was like that … always there when you needed a hug, a smile, a favor, or a smart-ass remark, particularly the smart-ass remark.

Sometime later Mandy Seaton invaded, arms full of shopping bags (she always had two or three bags cluttered with books, soft sculpture sewing craft gear, food and God knows what) and wearing a big straw hat. Jillian detached herself from Robin and me and threw herself into Mandy's arms.

"He's really dead," Jillian said in her quietest voice. "Tom's dead, Mandy!" She sobbed soundlessly, her shoulders doing little jumps.

Jillian and Mandy were about the same height, but where Jill was broad boned at cheek, shoulder and hip, Mandy was delicate, almost frail. And like most of the women of the COSS, Mandy's beauty was unconventional. Her hair was raven black and butt length. She wore round granny glasses and her teeth were crooked, so her smile was always lopsided, but she smiled often and caused others to do so too.

"What happened?" Mandy asked.

Jill's head had knocked Mandy's glasses askew; the two stood locked in an embrace. I leaned forward and extended a finger to slip the glasses back up the bridge of Mandy's nose.

Our eyes met. Hers were dark and large, like kewpie doll eyes. The kind that could keep your soul warm through the coldest winter of discontent.

"The cops said it looked like he fell out of the fifth-story window, probably during an asthma attack. Leaned out to get air, they said. Either that or he jumped." I heard myself saying. "The cops said it was the only one open, and the roof door was locked from inside."

Robin and Lily absently moved toward the front door, hugged, and left an arm around each other's waists. I suddenly became conscious that I was the only one in the room not being held and the non-contact was intense and lonely.

"Without Tom, I don't want to stay in this damn place ever again." Jillian said, looking around at the room as if seeing it for the first time. "I don't want to live without him. Oh God, he's dead."

She hugged Mandy more tightly, who in turn looked to me with an expression that was eloquent in its silence and we both understood: *there was no real solace to be given.*

"Jill, you'll stay with Don and me," Mandy said with quiet certainty. She looked at Lily. "Did you pack some things?"

"All done," Lily said, producing an overnight bag. Jillian suddenly turned away from Mandy and reached out to close my big hands with her two little ones.

"Don't leave me, Eric," she pleaded.

"I won't leave you," I whispered. "I won't."

All the way downstairs and out the front door she clung tightly to my side like a child on her first day off to school. Lily had called a car service, and it was waiting at the curb. Mandy got in first, somehow fitting all her bags and the bag we'd packed for Jillian in as well. Then Jill got in, somewhat clumsily because she still held both my hands.

I squeezed in last. As I reached to pull the door closed, I spotted the little girl in the pink jumpsuit.

She ran laughing and squealing past the front of the building. She held a stuffed animal in one hand and a water pistol in the other. Two of her little playmates chased in hot pursuit. They looked happy, completely caught up in the moment. I slammed the door, and we pulled away from the curb.

Mandy and Don's apartment was a big pre-war, six-room prop-warehouse off Eastern Parkway that sported a huge foyer. Hanging from a plant hook to the left of the door was Mr. Bones, a human skeleton from a doctor's office—the first sign that you were entering an unusual realm. It was dressed in a red cape and held a cup hilt rapier. A sign hung around his neck that said, "Abandon hope all ye who enter."

A series of Sherlock Holmes paintings (one of them featuring Mr. Bones), done by Don for a book publisher, lined the right wall. Mandy led us past the dinette into a living room packed with books to overflowing like Jillian and Tom's place had been. It was a consistent feature of the homes of all the Swan members.

"Clear off a space on the couch," Mandy said. "I'll make some tea." We emptied the books from the couch onto two jungle wicker chairs decked with politically incorrect real zebra skins.

Jillian nestled in next to me on the couch, quietly distant, leaning her head on my shoulder. She held onto my right arm, and when I shifted position to be comfortable she made a tiny, strangled sound, afraid I was leaving.

"I'm here, Jill," I said, hearing a strange numbness in my own voice. "I'm not going anywhere."

Don's Persian cat, Genghis, walked disdainfully into the room, checked us out with a glance, then wandered off. It was enough of a reminder that I hadn't taken anything for my allergies since the morning. I dry-popped a Sudafed from my belt pouch.

The action, so second nature to me when visiting any of my cat-owning friends, was suddenly a gauge of normalcy, against which all that had happened in the last three hours could be measured.

When Mandy entered the room with the tea, Jill was well into another intense crying jag. Mandy sat patiently, offering neither false consolation nor pointless small talk, waiting for the tears to spend themselves. She poured our tea and served it, letting her calm be an anchor for both of us.

"Tell me about the Renaissance festival, Eric," Mandy said. "Don said you started rehearsals last week."

"Yeah," I said, thankful for something concrete to focus on. "And Smitty is my assistant again."

"The skinny one with the great smile?" Mandy interjected.

"That's the guy, the mad juggler."

Smitty did a solo juggling act at the Faire and had gotten hooked on the stage combat bug two years ago because it involved partnering (fighting by yourself gets you put away). It paid a weekly salary (albeit small) and, Smitty said, he liked it "because fighters got lots of dates." He was really shy. His manual dexterity made him a natural stage fighter, and his personality was a pleasure to have at any show.

"Anyway," I continued, "we finished the first rehearsal week. I figured we were gonna have a great show, or at least, we did. Now, I don't know if I can stay with it...."

"Don't back out," Jill said between gulps of air from her sobbing. "Tom ... Tom would want you to keep going. It's your big break. You both talked about it so much."

"Jill" I said gasping for air a bit myself, "I jus—"

"You have to do the fight work, Eric. It's what you were meant to do. Tom calls you the 'Gene Kelly of combat'—" She stopped, caught her breath like someone who'd been running hard. "He *used* to call you that. Don't let your chance go. He used to tell me the same thing about my writing. He kept me writing when I had doubts about having something to really say. I used to write for him to read." She paused and looked distractedly around the room. "Who will I write for now?"

Neither of us had an answer for her that would have mattered. All I could do was hug her a little closer.

We said nothing.

Jill's talk of stage fighting made me think of the real stuff. "I have to call A.C. at the school." Jill squeezed me again and then unwrapped herself from me.

"Use the phone in the kitchen," Mandy said as slipped into the seat beside Jillian. When I left the room Jill was holding on tight, and Mandy was softly humming an old Irish love tune.

"Yes!" A.C.'s voice sounded gruff when he answered the phone. He always said, "Yes!" Never "Hello" or "A.C. here." A real natural for thug material.

"It's Eric, A.C."

"Hey, Zorro," he said. "What's up? You gonna weasel out on class again?"

"I'm glad I got you and not the machine," I said, trying to find the right words. They weren't become any easier with the reiteration. "Tom De Dannin is dead."

"Shit!" his voice dropped an octave. "What happened?"

"We don't really know yet, he fell from the fifth floor into the courtyard. I—I found him." I was gulping air now and feeling a little dizzy as I spoke. "I'm with Jillian over at Mandy Seaton's."

"What can I do?" That was A.C. too, no bullshit, no false comfort, just ready to do what needed to be done. Like Tom, he was the definition of a friend.

"Nothing, not right now, but I may need you to deal with the "blurocracy" for Jillian's sake. Obviously, they won't show in court today. Maybe you can get Poppo out in Coney Island to make some calls."

"No sweat," he answered. A long pause ran on for several seconds that felt like minutes. The background noise on the phone was thunderous against the silence. I could still hear Mandy humming in the living room.

"What happened that made him fall from a building?" A.C. asked. "Were you guys rehearsing a stunt or something?" I could hear that he hated to ask.

"No, I was in the apartment," I said flatly. "I don't know what happened." Even as I said it, I thought, *what a lame thing to say.*

Somewhere in the back of my mind there was a wrongness about his death calling to me, but the phantom voice was so faint.

"Do you want me to send everybody home from your stunt combat class?"

Monday nights, I taught unarmed combat and tumbling for stage at A.C.'s martial arts school. I'd taken the last week off for the faire rehearsal.

"No." My voice sounded strange. "Smitty said he'd stop by. If he does, ask him to run 'em through the last rapier fight we did a couple of weeks ago to review."

"And if he doesn't show?"

"Then maybe you can just work them through basic falls and throws."

A.C. confined himself to the real thing when it came to fighting, and while it meant he knew nothing about Western-style swashbuckling, he knew a hell of a lot about falling down safely, hence the occasional stunt work.

"No problem," he said. "I'll be here all night anyway. Stop by on your way home."

"I'll stay here tonight for Jill."

"Yeah. Makes sense. I gotta get back to a private student," A.C. said. "You need anything, you call, doesn't matter what time."

"Is she pretty?" I said with a ghost of a smile, the first I'd had all day.

"You know it." He gave an evil chuckle. Then his voice got serious. "You okay, man?"

I took a long time to reply. "No, but that's the way it goes."

"*Imjun motae*," he quoted to me in Korean. "Courage not to retreat. Keep strong!" It was a teacher thing to say, but I knew he meant it because he lived it.

"I'll do my best," I said and hung up. I stood in the kitchen for a full five minutes as I concentrated on deep breathing to gather myself again for Jill.

When I entered the living room, both Don and Robin had arrived and were sitting on the wicker chairs facing Mandy and Jill on the couch. Don was a little guy, five foot five and slight of build, with delicate features and a long, thin face. I didn't know him as well as I knew most of the Silver Swan crowd.

"Hey, Eric," Don said. He stood to give me his chair, but I nodded him off and went to sit on the floor near Jillian. As I passed Don, I got that feeling I often do when I stand close to other men. I become acutely aware of just how much larger in scale I am. It spooks even me sometimes.

Jillian reached out and clamped a hand on my shoulder. I curled my hand around hers.

"Robin and Lily took Pyewacket and Corwin to Lily's," Jill said in a quiet but steady voice. "Lily went to identify Tom's body so you wouldn't have to." Her eyes searched mine.

"I brought some KFC and soda," Robin said, offering me a bucket of the Colonel's best. I declined.

I noticed from the smell that Robin had also brought some whiskey for Jillian. It was her favorite hard liquor, and we all knew she'd have major need of it. Even though Jill often had some sort of allergy drug or other in her system, we knew she was clean at the moment, and the whisky would do the work of tranquilizers. I turned my head away from the smell—I, the son of an alcoholic, and even the smell of the stuff turns my stomach—made it a bitch to be a bouncer in the East Village.

"Eat some food, Eric," Mandy said, seeing my distaste at the smell. "You know you're useless when your blood sugar drops." She smiled, and I had no power to resist.

Three pieces of chicken later, I had to admit I'd been hungry. Half a dozen people dropped by. Patrick, Neville, and others all brought food and friendship for Jill.

Around seven o'clock, Lily Chan came in with some Chinese food and ice cream for me and Jillian.

"They have Tom in the basement of Kings County Hospital," she said after Jillian had pressed her for details. She dished out the food. "Like they're ashamed to have a morgue. Tom was on a steel table covered by a sheet in this little cubicle-type room."

We were still sitting in the living room, though it was starting to look like a delicatessen.

"I had to identify my dad there," I said, "through that scratched up Plexiglas window, under those fluorescent lights. It was after the car hit him. The whole thing felt so cheap." I knocked back a straight-up Classic Coke and round myself thinking of offering one to Tom before I caught myself.

"At least on *Quincy* they use a TV hook-up so they don't have to do it face to face," Lily said.

I could still picture my dad on the metal table. Even cold and dead, the bloating from the booze was plainly visible. The thought made me acutely aware, once again, of the whiskey fumes around me, and I felt vaguely nauseous.

"How ... how did he look?" Jill asked.

"At peace," Lily said in a quiet voice. She took great care not to let Jill see the lie in her eyes. "He even still seemed to be smiling." Jill just nodded as if some deep question had been answered.

The phone rang, and Lily popped up with "I'll get it" — apparently glad to be away from the responsibility of memory — and went into the kitchen. We sat in silence a moment, each of us picturing Tom on that cold slab and trying to reconcile it with our image of the alive, active Tom.

"I'm a mess," Jill said suddenly. She ran her fingers through her hair, tugging on snags. "Could I take a bath?" She sounded like a child who'd spilled chocolate syrup on a new dress.

"Of course you can." Mandy hurried across the room and took her hand. "Robin, will you go run the water while we pick out bath oil?" She helped Jill to her feet, then Mandy and Robin steered her out of the room.

I was abruptly very alone.

I collapsed like a deflated balloon, all the energy gone from my arms and legs. I didn't have the strength to pick up the glass of soda, to stand, or to think. All the events of the day got hazy, and even though I sat slumped on the couch, I felt as if I might fall over.

"Tom, you son of a bitch," I whispered, "What are we gonna do without you?"

That was how Mandy found me ten minutes later, still staring straight ahead; empty.

She sat next to me. "Eric, are you okay?"

I stared at her dumbfounded for a moment. "I'm numb, Mandy. My best friend's dead and I don't … I can't even cry." She looked at me with eyes older than water.

"Give it time, Eric. You're in shock. There will be tears and pain and grieving."

Her voice was so musical, contained such a calming quality, that even if she hadn't been making sense, I would have listened. "For now, Jill needs you to be calm," she continued, "and you are." She patted my hand and, using her Jewish grandmother's accent, she said, "Trust me, tears you'll shed."

I didn't laugh, but it got a smile out of me. Then she shrugged her shoulders just right and a laugh came, strained and half-choked but a real laugh.

"It's the best medicine, Eric," she said. "It's all that kept me goin' when things went sour with my first husband, Ruff."

"It just feels … I don't know … sacrilegious to even think about laughing."

"It isn't," she said firmly. "She'll need it, we all will. After the numbness goes, when the feelings come full-blown, one of them has to be humor. Think about Tom's smart-alec view on things."

I reached over to pat her hand. "You know, I love you, lady," I said, "and given half a chance, if the timing had been right after Ruff …" I paused and sighed theatrically. "I sure could've 'lusted' you."

She smiled her cockeyed grin where one tooth peeked out over her lip. She was every bit inscrutable in the smile that followed. "That, in a nutshell, is the secret of the human comedy—timing!"

Jillian found the two of us laughing when she returned with Robin, and the rest of the evening went much easier. We sat around 'til one a.m. telling bawdy Tom stories, singing ribald songs and spiking most of Jillian's beverages. Calls came in all night too, some directly for Jill, some for Mandy in hopes of finding Jill.

Tom and Jill had a vast network of SF fan and medieval recreationist friends. The news of Tom's death had raced across the country like wildfire. Mandy and Lily took most of the calls and during the course of them, plans for Tom's funeral began to take shape. A bagpiper from Connecticut who'd met Tom at the Scottish Games two years ago would come and pipe Tom across. Two Wiccan priestesses and an Episcopal bishop who knew Tom and Jill from a country dance group agreed to officiate jointly. People from as far away as California would be flying or driving in for next Saturday's service.

Outside of the arrangements, the calls were about two things: Was Jillian all right and how had Tom died?

People stopped calling around midnight, and by one o'clock only Mandy, Don, Jill, Lily and I were left. Lily wanted to give up her room for Jillian. Jill wouldn't have it, so Mandy made up a guest futon in her sewing room for her.

I suggested making up the couch in the living room for me, but Jill wouldn't hear of it. She wanted me with her, so I settled down on the futon, kicked my shoes off and functioned as a warming stone for Jillian.

She wrapped herself around me and held on truly for dear life. "Thank you, Mandy," Jill said in a polite voice. "You've been so kind."

"Nonsense, Jill," Mandy said quite seriously. "Nothing any of us could do would be enough." Jill reached up and kissed her tenderly on the lips and the two women embraced. When they parted Mandy leaned over and planted a kiss on my forehead.

"Timing," she whispered with a sly smirk.

With a final "Good night," Mandy clicked off the overhead light and was gone. Then I was alone with Jill.

She was quiet for a time, her head resting against my heart, her arms around me. I thought that maybe she would fall asleep, but then she asked, "Eric, why did my Tom die today?"

I had no answer but I felt I had to say something. "If there is a God, Jill, there is a reason, but I sure as hell don't know what that could be."

"I wish it had been me instead," she said.

I felt my throat go tight, and I thought, *At last I can cry for you, Tom,* but my eyes stayed dry.

"No, Jillian, don't say that ... don't even think that." I stroked her hair absently as if she had been a cat. "You know he couldn't have made it without you. You've always been the stronger one."

"But the pain, Eric. It's like broken glass in my heart. I just want to die."

"I know," I said, "I know. But ... you have to keep going, you have to finish *Silken Thomas,* and to write all those stories you've planned and told Tom and me about. With time, the edges of glass will dull. They may never go away ... never ... but you'll live with it the way you live with other losses. You live for who is left."

I listened to myself pep talk Jillian. *What bullshit is this? He's fuckin' dead. Out the window and splat! Twenty-seven hard-earned years of life over, and it makes no sense! He didn't die saving somebody from a fire, or get in a bar fight or damn ... like he should have ... in a sword fight with Odin on his lips and with a snarl of defiance. He died like an unwanted puppy dropped out a window.*

"I'm glad you're here, Eric," she said after a time. "You're a good friend to Tom."

"I wish Tom were here instead of me, hon," I said. "He'd know what to do."

Jill just nodded and wept a little more.

Much later, we lay quiet, Jill pressed against me, her breathing regular and the night air was still. Occasionally, sounds drifted in from Newkirk Avenue: a train rumble, a loud radio with some Latin tune, a car horn.

I'd taken off my shirt and socks but kept on my sweatpants. Jill wore an old-fashioned nightshirt. Sleep seemed a thousand years distant for me. I kept seeing Tom's face lying on that concrete; his eyes that used to sparkle haunted me—so empty of life, and energy—so dead.

"Eric," Jill's voice seemed tiny and far away. She hadn't been asleep after all.

"I'm here, Jill."

"Make love to me."

"What?"

"I need to know I'm alive," she said. "Need to know I want to be."

I looked down at her head resting on my chest, just a dark shape. I was suddenly aware of her body heat through the sheet that separated us and the floral scent of the bath oils and shampoo.

"Tom used to kid me all the time," she said in that same tiny, far away voice. "About how much you and I flirted."

He'd used to kid me too, made a point of reminding me that Jill and he had an "open" marriage. But she'd never exercised her options with anyone, let alone me. As much as I was part of the free-wheeling lifestyle of the Renaissance faire world I wasn't really all that comfortable with "poaching"—even with permission.

"I think it's always been more fun to dance around it," I whispered to Jill's dark shape … and to Tom's imagined image, too.

"And you have your own code about territorial rights."

It was the first hint of humor I'd heard in her voice since the afternoon. "Yeah." I breathed.

She shifted beside me, and I knew she was looking up at me. I could feel the power of that stare and the smell of her beneath the scent of the rose scented bath gel was suddenly strong.

"We were both silly and both right," she said with more strength than I'd heard in her voice all day. "You never could have been a danger to Tom and me; no one could. And it's a moot point now. I'm going to be alone for a long time." My pulse quickened now, my breathing shallow.

"The pagans call lovemaking 'The Great Ritual,'" Jill said. "The ultimate prayer." I reached down and pulled her up on my body, enfolding her in my arms and kissing her with reverent passion. We rolled over, became entangled in the sheets (I remember thinking how much like a shroud they were) and worked our way free of them without breaking the kiss.

It was odd. I felt the passion clearly enough. My body responded directly to the stimuli of her touch, her smell, her taste. Of course, I was hyper-aware of Jill, both that it was her, specifically with all the memories that entailed, and that she was a bridge to a time and a circumstance that would never be again.

All the physicality was there, the release from the horrid pressure of the day, the pent-up desire, deflected by our sense of propriety and Puritan values, the sheer need to escape. It was all there and yet, it was not about pleasure. Neither mine nor hers, though in truth I think there was a great deal of that for both of us. It really was a prayer, a hymn to that fierce, crazed, loving, childish, trustworthy punk we both loved.

When I reached for the condoms I always carried in hope in my belt pouch, she held my hand.

"If anything comes of this," she said in church tones, "it'll be Tom's last gift to both of us."

We made fierce, passionate, life-affirming love, and I cried through all of it, silent tears that seemed to never end.

I was still crying at dawn with Jill wrapped in my arms, sleeping the sleep of the exhausted. By then, I was sure there had been three souls in the bed all night.

Amen.

Chapter Seven

On Saturday, they put Tom's shell in the ground to the accompaniment of bagpipes. Over a hundred people were there to witness it, but I wasn't one of them. I couldn't. I can't stand funerals—not for people I care about. So Friday afternoon I left New York on an Amtrak train to Wilmington, Delaware, to visit Kyrstal, whom I hadn't seen in two months.

"Jesus, Eric," Krystal said after the first fierce hug of greeting at the station platform. "You look like hell!"

"Hello," I answered. "I look like hello." She smiled at that, a wide amiable smile that went all the way to her eyes.

"I assume food is your second priority," she said with certainty. Krystal Collins was as petite as I was big, barely five feet and built like a little boy with her jet-black hair cut in a retro Dorothy Hamill cut. Even with her on tiptoes I bent almost double to give her a long, passionate kiss that put us in danger of breaking public decency laws by the time we came up for air.

"Whoa, sailor," she gasped. "Let's get you home before you're arrested as a pervert."

I caught sight of us reflected in the windows of the food concession and noticed that, aside from how haggard I looked, Kryss looked like a preteen next to me.

At twenty-seven and divorced, she always had to carry ID to pass as adult. We'd met the year before when she was Peter Pan to my Captain Hook in a regional production.

"Okay, Little Peter, I'll keep my hands off 'til we're in the car."

61

"Oh no, Big Peter," she said, grabbing my hand and leading me out of the station to her car. "You'll keep your hands off until I get us home. I get too distracted to drive!" She owned an old Ford LTD, a regular land yacht. It didn't have bucket seats, and since she had to have the front seat all the way up for her to drive, I had to sit in the back seat if I didn't want to eat my knees.

"So," she said as she pulled the car out of the underpass parking spot, "Now's your chance to tell me all about it!" I stared out the car window as downtown Wilmington flew by, and we got onto 95 South. It was a good ten minutes of Kryss's small talk to draw me out enough to speak. Even then, it came out tersely in small spurts of description, often in answer to a prodding question. I talked about Tom and Jillian until we hit the outskirts of Newark, Delaware.

At a stop light, she turned to look at me and said, "Okay, this weekend is for you to forget. Just you, me and all the ice cream you can eat. Mourn Tom later; for now, relax."

In Newark, Krystal stopped at the dance school, where she was ballet mistress, to teach her Friday classes. I watched while Kryss led her twelve- and thirteen-year-old charges through a warm-up. Most of the girls were as tall as or taller than Kryss, and it was amusing to watch her work them like a pixie drill sergeant.

After a while I wandered into one of the smaller studios that Kryss had told me would be empty for the evening and closed the door behind me.

I turned the boom box on, popped in one of Kryss's driving tapes and stepping to the beat, did my best to sweat the jangled nervous energy out of me so I didn't kill Kryss when we finally got into bed.

Normally, I hate to work out to music, preferring to listen to my body's own natural rhythms, but right then it was the last thing I wanted to do. For the last four days I'd done virtually nothing but sit around with Jill, forced to feel my own body's rhythms with no break.

I'd slept with Jill each night, but with no repeat of our midnight passion. Neither of us ever mentioned it again.

I had done none of my usual morning workouts, martial classes or weight training during this time. I was feeling ten years older, horribly sedentary, and felt ready to primal scream myself into a coma.

I needed to exercise some demons.

For a warm-up, I did five hundred cruncher sit-ups, three hundred pushups, fifteen minutes of shadow boxing, and fifteen minutes of skipping rope. That got a sweat going.

Then I stretched: legs, back, groin, arms, and neck. After that I felt awake, so I started my fencing drills, holding my arm out with an imaginary sword. Fifty lunges on each leg. Then I recreated some of the fights I'd choreographed over the last year. That was my way of making practice forms for the Western sword.

I was pleasantly exhausted after a half hour of that. It was draining since I imagined a real opponent for each cut and parry. That kind of concentration takes a lot out of a guy.

In my mind, I could hear A.C.'s voice leading his class: "When you're tired is the best time to practice. Let the ki power take over. Be strong!"

So I kept going. I shifted gears and started on my eastern martial arts regimen. I did the Tai Chi Chuan short form twice, forcing myself to slow down and breathe correctly to let the power flow. As my grand finale I was ready for the heavy stuff—my Hwa Rang Do forms.

There are nine forms to black belt level, each more complex and intricate than the last. I'd only made it halfway to blue belt, but four forms were enough. At the end of an hour I was drenched in sweat, and so beat I could hardly stand.

That's when Krystal poked her head in. She took one look at me and smiled. "Okay, food is now top priority, but you shower before you get in my car!" She threw me a towel and pointed to the school's dressing room where the instructors had a shower stall. The hot water beating on my sore muscles felt like heaven, and by the time I dressed in fresh clothes, I felt almost human.

Kryss kept up with me bite for bite at dinner, which shouldn't be physically possible considering I consumed nearly her weight in food. Later, she outdistanced me in bed, showing the enthusiasm and athleticism that had made the run of *Peter Pan* one of the best experiences of my life.

"Oh my God," I said as I lay back on her platform bed hours later, soaked with a whole new layer of sweat that was earned the hard way.

"You're gonna kill me!" She chuckled gleefully and crouched naked on the edge of the bed like a tyro gargoyle.

"If you can't stand the heat, stay out of my oven!" Naked, she looked the part of a woman instead of a little girl, albeit a woman formed in perfect miniature. She crawled up beside me and nestled in the hollow of my left arm with an impish expression on her face. She signed and snuggled against me and I nuzzled my chin on her forehead.

"Why the hell do you have to live so far away?"

"You're the one who lives far away," she said, "I grew up near here. I have the school and the dance company here."

"I know, Hon, but … shit—"

She reached a finger to shush me without looking and poked me in the nose, which did the job of stopping me woolgathering. "I'm here because I have to be," Kryss said. "You're in New York because you have to be. It's worked for over a year. Don't jinx it."

"It's just that seeing Jill after Tom … it, it—"

"Reminds you of mortality, impermanence, and all that," she concluded for me.

"Well, yeah."

"And you're looking to grab onto something, or someone, you can hold onto."

"No, uh …"

"Don't lie. You're grasping at straws, Eric," she said with a firm voice. "I'll be a love toy for you, hon, but I won't be a straw or a punching bag."

"You'd be a speed bag anyway, toots."

She crawled up onto my chest to stare me in the eyes. "Don't correct me when I'm being profound." It was awfully hard for her to look terribly menacing with her hair in a mess and pouting, but she tried. Her knees were squeezing the air out of my chest.

"Sorry, Little Peter, but you're also right." I wrapped my arms around her and squeezed some air out of her. "I've been working hard not to do this straw grasping thing since my own divorce five years ago. It's just … well, Tom … uh … threw me off."

"Well?" She lowered her head until she was nose to nose with me.

"Well, you did say something about 'love toy'?"

We stayed in bed till Saturday afternoon, leaving once only briefly for brunch at a place called The Country Pantry. Out front stood a ten-foot-tall papier mâché Amish farmer holding a sign that read "Goot Food." Before we arrived back at the apartment we bought ice cream, bananas and chocolate syrup.

We next came up for air well after dark.

"That's it," Kryss said as she came out of the bathroom. She wore one of my Fightmasters Association t-shirts. On her, it was a nightgown. "It hurts to piss," she complained. "It's time for you to find another hobby."

"You could get fat and ugly to repel me," I suggested. "I'll go out and buy some pound cake to eat. Other than that, if I'm locked in a room with you—"

"Then we go out!"

We did.

Krystal took me to a roadhouse/dance club in Smyrna called "Loonies." It was a chameleon of a place, probably a dive bar at the start that went disco, country western and then hip-hop as the decades sped by. It retained design elements from each period in its décor—which is to say it was now a dive with a mirrored ball, long horns on the wall, a garish paint job and a sunken dance floor.

"Charming place," I yelled down at her as we moved up to the bar. Kryss stood on the brass rail to be able to call the bartender.

"One rum and Coke and one plain Coke," she ordered.

The bartender looked at her oddly but filled the order pointedly pushing the plain Coke in front of Krystal. She smiled sweetly, picked up the rum and Coke from in front of me and chugalugged it. "One more please!" she said sweetly. He started to say something but I leaned in.

"She's twenty-seven, Mack. The bouncer checked." He looked at the bouncer, who had been waiting for this. He knew Kryss as a semi-regular. She got her second R&C.

"I love morons," Kryss said when we finally settled at a table overlooking the dance floor.

"That's good, because there are so many to choose from."

"I'm almost used to it," she said philosophically. "I know I'll be carded until I'm a grandmother."

"I haven't been carded since I was twelve," I said with a satisfied smile.

"Oh, shut up."

We watched the dance floor for a while and enjoyed dishing the locals. "Look at that fine specimen," I said to Kryss pointing to a particularly thuggish type coming in the door.

Dressed in a denim work shirt and polyester checkered pants was a six-foot, 240-pound ex-college football type gone a little soft around the middle.

"He's probably named Bubba."

"That one's bad news, Eric," she said when she saw my grin of dismissal as I watched "Bubba." "He and his pals started trouble here a couple of times."

True to form Bubba was already arguing with the bouncer but after a couple of back-and-forth moments was allowed into the club with a couple of friends.

"Just like when I was bouncing at the Tavern in the East Village; makes me nostalgic for home. Not!" I whispered.

The rest of the roadhouse crew was an odd mix of post-college, yuppie and fringe country western types, most of them five to ten years younger than my thirty-five. The clothes style ranged from drop-dead disco chic to go-to-hell redneck denim. Jeans not allowed, please.

"My gosh, Eric, it's true," Krystal suddenly exclaimed in horror, after watching the dance floor for several dances "White people have absolutely no natural rhythm!"

"Now, now," I assured her, "that's racist. Maybe all people in Delaware have no rhythm. I see no African-Americans currently on the floor."

"I'm from Delaware, and I have rhythm," Krystal protested.

"But you're not on the dance floor." I finished my Coke with a flourish.

"Oh my!" she feigned terror. "I must uphold the honor of my state!"

"Allow me to help you, madam!"

"Ever the knight errant, sir," she said with a slight bow.

I took her hand and off we went.

Delaware and the white man's rhythmic honor were upheld that night at Loonies. We burned up the dance floor and terrified the natives with seeming ease.

Dance lifts are fun as hell with a hundred-and-one-pound partner! We took breaks whenever my lungs gave out. Regardless of the level of fitness I maintained Krystal was capable of literally dancing rings around me but was kind and sat down with me. She could have gone the whole night without a break.

At one point I collapsed into a chair while she kindly took the one beside me.

"You really should have been a dancer," she said.

"Not if all dance teachers are as tough as you." My shirt was soaked with sweat, and you could practically see the waves of heat rolling off me but it felt good.

"I'm serious," she said, punching me in the arm.

"Ow! Seriously, if I'd gotten into movement a couple of years sooner, it could have happened." I drained my Coke. "I wear tights as much as I would have at the Kirov, but I'd miss the clatter of the steel there."

"Well, you handle a woman like you do a sword," she whispered, leaning in conspiratorially. "Gently, skillfully and with a sort of ..." She made a circle of her hand, looking for a word.

"Respect and reverence" I suggested, "as befits a fine, deadly weapon." She rolled her eyes and gave me a look.

"You're hopeless. You want another soda?" She stood up.

"Thanks, but you'd better ease up on the rums, I may be the 'designated driver' but remember, I'm from New York. I don't have a driver's license!"

"The last two I brought were sans rum, cupcake."

She walked off into the crowd, and I once more admired her cute little butt that was barely concealed by her leather mini-dress. *Man,* I thought, *how the hell do I deserve that much woman? And she's smarter than me to boot!*

Sitting there drenched once more in sweat, catching my breath, I made the mistake of relaxing. That's when I thought about Tom.

Krystal had done an amazing job of keeping me solidly in the present. I'd only thought of Tom and Jill once in an hour. Now, the flood of memories came, full strength like a tidal wave of emotion.

"It comes down to every man needing something to believe in," Tom said to me. We were sitting in a hotel bar in Boston during a science fiction convention. Tom was in full black Elizabethan garb with Courage on his hip. I was dressed as a Hollywood swashbuckler in blue. I'd just done a lecture demo on the sword styles in fantasy books,

Tom always dressed that way at conventions. Of course, he still wore his beret.

"What do you mean?" I asked.

"Well, like, A.C. has his Hwa Rang Do," Tom said. "That's the cornerstone of his life. All his decisions are based on that. For me, it's Jillian. Back in the gang days, my only thought was of day-to-day survival, and even that—only half-hearted. But Jill, she made it worth staying alive and thinking about tomorrow." He threw back the plastic cup of Jack Daniels he held in his hand and gave me that Rod Serling tight-lipped smile that earned him the street name "Grinner."

"Then, I guess it's acting for me," I said, trying to be profound and philosophical while eyeing a young, shapely woman made up as a Klingon three tables away.

"No way, man," Tom insisted, "the acting is just an excuse for you to handle swords. Face it, that's your religion, man, the way of the sword." He smiled smugly, like he always did when he was sure he'd hit on a truth of the universe. "Doesn't matter what culture or style, swords turn you on like a good woman does most men."

"Nah." I tried hard not to acknowledge what I was wearing. "I didn't pick up a sword 'til three years after college. I was already working as an actor while I was in school."

"That's crap. I was in love with Jillian before I ever met her. You were a rapier junky before you ever saw one. The old nature versus nurture theory proven out." I glanced at Courage on Tom's hip and realized my pulse raced

*the same way when I saw the clean symmetry of its hilt as when I looked at
the shapely Klingon.*

"I hate it when you're right, Tom."

"Love you too, brother." *He grinned wider and waved a salute from his
"Free Ireland" pin.*

The memory faded into the background. "Goddamn it, Tom," I
cursed, wiping tears from my eyes. "I should have gone first; Jill needs
you." I searched the dance floor crowd to locate Krystal. "Why the
fuck did you have to go first? I'd always expected you and Jill would
do my eulogy after some asshole special effects man blew me up on
some crap like *Igor and the Lunatics Part Three.*"

A commotion at the bar drew my focus. Some cow-like creature
that seemed to have been stuffed into a hot-pink sheath dress was
screaming loudly at Krystal in an almost human voice. The creature
must have had its horns concealed under a hair-sprayed tangle of
"frosted" fake blonde hair and was dolled up with a big butterfly pin
hovering on her massive left breast.

"Stop making eyes at him you little tramp," the creature bellowed
in an alcohol-dulled voice. "He's my boyfriend." She would have
towered over Krystal even without the three-inch stiletto spike heels,
but she was pressing in on Kryss and leaning over, attempting to
intimidate the smaller woman.

I say attempting, because Kryss used to be a civilian worker for the
NYPD at the Central Park Station and there are still TAC sergeants
who wet themselves when her name is mentioned. Kryss was at a
disadvantage, however, because both her hands held drinks and her
back was to the bar.

I jumped up and headed over. The scene was beginning to draw
quite a crowd, and to coin a phrase, "The crowd was getting ugly."

"Please get out of my way," Krystal said calmly but in a firm voice.
"I am not interested in your boyfriend."

"Don't lie to me, bitch," the creature said, pointing a Lee Press-on
nail at Krystal. "I saw you staring at him."

"He was staring at me while I ordered my drinks," Krystal said in
a very flat, still firm voice. I'd only heard that tone once from Kryss,

when a guest male dancer had talked back to her in front of the company. The last day he worked for that dance company, as I recall.

The "hunk" of a boyfriend was the redneck I'd nicknamed Bubba. He was making mumbling noises and grabbing at the creature, trying to draw its focus from Krystal. The bouncer, a college kid and a wrestler from the look of his neck, had stepped in and was trying to sort it all out.

I was close enough now so I could see the troweled-on makeup and false eyelashes on the Creature, and the thought of Bubba and it breeding sent a momentary chill down my spine.

I could understand Bubba staring at Kryss. I almost felt sorry for him. The creature, on the other hand, was waving that press-on claw in Krystal's face and continuing to squawk. The disco lights reflecting off the rhinestones in the butterfly pin made it appear to be fluttering over a huge pink hill.

"It's little ass flashin' sluts like you that always cause the trouble," it said. Then it made the big mistake. It poked one of the press-on claws right into Krystal's right breast. Hard.

WUMP! Kryss leaned back against the bar and kicked with her right leg, catching the creature square between its udders. It was a hard kick that sent the vision in pink reeling back into two innocent bar patrons. They didn't go down, but the Creature ended up on its butt.

"Oh shit," I thought. I moved through the crowd, most of whom were now laughing, and got right up beside Kryss.

"Here's your Coke, Big Peter." she said with a nonplussed expression.

"Geez, Li'l Pete," I whispered, "Let's get out of here before—"

Bubba and the bouncer went to try and pick up the Creature, who was screaming and pointing at Krystal. Bubba looked up at Krystal, but I could see the confusion register on his face. Good Ole boys can't hit a woman, but here was *his* woman on her huge behind and the culprit was a woman!

The bouncer gave Kryss a look of "get out of here" which she acknowledged with a nod.

"Okay, let's go, now," she said.

I moved to Krystal, grabbing her arm, but it was too late.

Bubba threw a sucker punch right into the bouncer for "manhandling my woman" and then stood up, his gaze fixed on me as a viable alternative target to Kryss.

"Get to the car," I urged Kryss. She started to protest, but Bubba cut her off.

"You gonna pay for what been done to Eunice, asshole!" Bubba declared. "Get him, boys."

Eunice?

Bubba, being a man of action, had made all the speeches he was going to make. He came for me, and I could see he wasn't alone.

Two others separated themselves from the crowd: a bald-headed guy a bit shorter than him wearing a string cowboy tie, and another six-footer with blond hair and a thick mustache.

Krystal backed off.

I glance over my left shoulder to see her setting the drinks on the bar to free her hands. On the floor the bouncer moaned, all but senseless from the blindsiding.

I made one last attempt to hold off the violence. "This can all be talked out. No need for anybody to get hurt," I said, with my hands spread and a big smile on my face but Bubba wasn't having any of it.

He came at me like a bull, making the same mistake most people make who haven't seen me move. They think, *He's huge, broad, slow as a truck*, and figure they can outmaneuver me.

Wrong.

Bubba came in fast and tried to slip around to my left, intending to kidney punch me. I let him get to my left hip before I flicked out my left foot in a snap kick to his leading shin.

That put the hurt on him.

At the same time I drove the butt of my left elbow up under his chin, snapping his head back fast enough to knock his lights out.

His two friends watched him crumble, almost as stunned as he was.

I used that second of situation reversal to move in on them. I hit the bald one with a boring old front snap kick, planting my size fourteen dress shoe right at his sternum. I actually heard the snap of the breastbone before his back slammed into the bar, and he fell off the stool in a heap.

Number three had had time to soak it all in and was on his feet. He was four inches shorter than me, but with the solid body of an athlete and powerful legs that ended in steel-toed cowboy boots. Surprise wouldn't take him.

He settled into a martial arts stance that advertised he was a Chinese stylist and came at me with a flurry of high-low kicks intended to drive those steel boots an inch or two into me. I back-pedaled using a fencer's retreat step and used slap blocks to deflect the attack.

He tried to set me up in a pattern, high kick, high kick, low kick, so I would zig while he zagged and eat toe steel. But you can't kid a kidder, as my dad used to say, and to any fencer the second and third intention ploy is child's play.

Like a good chess player, swordsmen feint and counter-feint. When this guy kicked high on the third cycle of attacks (expecting me to go low), I did a two-footed jump forward (a demi-balestra, really), landing on his standing foot, grabbed his kicking leg at the knee and yanked up as hard as I could. This put him into a forced vertical 180-degree split.

This had two effects: first, it ripped the crotch of his jeans to shockingly reveal he wore no underwear, and second, it overstretched his groin muscle, ending his martial arts career for a good long time.

He dropped with a pitiful moan and lay on the floor in a heap. Less than a minute had gone by, but it felt like an hour to me. I was in that hyped-up, post-action adrenal rush that makes the whole world move in slow motion.

The bouncer was back on his feet by this time, close to me, ready to do his job but not sure who deserved his attention. Most of the crowd was more than ready to announce who had done what while the bouncer was in la la land.

Krystal interceded, spoke a few words to him and he stopped at a distance to keep an eye on all the players.

"Let's go," Kryss said to me, gripping my arm tightly. "Billy'll let us go and square it with the local cops. Nobody is hurt bad enough or has enough brains to sue you."

I let her guide me out through the crowd, vaguely aware of Eunice's squeals in the background of "Oh baby, what did that brute do to you?" as she knelt beside Bubba.

Outside the cool night air hit me like a slap. I suddenly got woozy and my knees went to Jello. Krystal supported me partway to the car, but I had to stop to throw up, using the back fender of somebody's pickup truck for support.

I thought, *Geez, this sort of shit was routine with you in the gangs, Tom. Except for that bodega thing. I haven't been in a real fight since high school.*

I was sick for a full five minutes. I kept seeing Eunice flopping around with her butterfly pin on a field of spandex and imagined Tom grinning at me like an idiot from beneath his beret. He would have loved to rib me about my Donnybrook.

I kept flashing on the image of the last time I'd seen him lying in that alley, still wearing that beret.

Beret!

I stood up so quickly, almost knocking Kryss over. I must have looked like a complete madman because she jumped back. "The pin was gone." I yelled at her. She looked at me oddly. "Tom's beret," I repeated. "His 'Free Ireland' pin was gone!"

"I'm telling you, A.C.," I practically yelled into Krystal's phone. "Tom didn't lean out a window to get some air and become 'overcome' with a spell of dizziness. And he didn't jump."

There was a static crackle from the other end. "You're really serious about this, aren't you?"

"Dead serious," I said. I had badgered Kyrstal with my "revelation" all the way home and insisted on calling A.C. immediately.

"Okay," A.C. said, "Poppo knows a lot of regular cops and can probably get a look at the file, but there's no way he can risk smuggling—"

"I don't need him to," I interrupted. "I just need him to check the photos of the scene and the evidence logs for that damn pin. It wasn't in the effects returned to Jillian. If it's there in the log then it was just an oversight and I'm wrong. If it's not—"

"If it's not, it's not," A.C. insisted. "All it means is that they missed it, or somebody stole it before the cops got there. This is New York, Eric."

"I don't know if I'm right," I insisted, "but just get him to do it, okay? I'll argue at you in person in two days."

"I'll get on the horn with him first thing tomorrow. Just do me a favor and don't go manufacturing facts."

"Yes, Mother," I assured him. "Thanks." I hung up slowly and stared at the phone. I turned to Krystal seated on a stool at her breakfast bar looking all the world like a pixie on a toadstool. She wore one of my t-shirts as a housedress and had her knees drawn up under her chin, which caused a tiny wisp of her pubic hair to peek out from between her muscular buns. She was staring at me hard.

"You think I'm crazy?"

She continued to stare which made me feel defensive.

"I know it sounds crazy." I removed myself from her stare and paced around her apartment still dressed in my dance clothes. "I mean, shit, people don't kill people you know, do they? That always happens to somebody else—like in some of the freakin' grade B movies I work on."

She just stared.

I finally stopped in front of her and looked her in the eyes again. "Kryss, am I out of my mind?"

"Well," she said thoughtfully, "probably, but that doesn't have much bearing on all this." She unfolded from the stool and walked toward me. My t-shirt hung to her knees. "I think, considering Tom's past and all, it's really a possibility."

"You mean an old score or something like that?" Even as I said it I realized it sounded like dialogue out of an old Monogram B-picture.

"Not necessarily, but possibly. It doesn't really matter what it was." She reached her arms around my waist.

"Why?" It was nice to be held but I was all thought at the moment, not in my body at all, so I didn't get the full effect of her breasts nuzzling my belly.

"Because," she said, looking up at me with a smile, "for the first time since you stepped off the train, you are acting, not reacting. Right or wrong, you are looking forward and not stuck in that horrible moment." She smiled all the way to her eyes, suddenly the goddamned sexiest pixie I'd ever seen.

"I … I guess you're right," I said quietly. "I do feel … uh, alive. Yeah … alive. Tom is dead, but I'm alive. Whatever the true story, whatever happened, I can find out." I put my arms around her shoulders with enough new enthusiasm to cause her to wince when I squeezed.

"Sorry," I said but when I tried to pull away she held me.

"It's okay, Big P. It's nice to feel you hugging me actively as opposed to reactively."

Perceptive little minx.

"Well, I could be more active, if there wasn't a moratorium on—"

She giggled evilly. "Somehow I don't feel as sore as before I saw you paste those Delmarva rednecks."

We spent several hours making her sorry she'd said that.

Sunday was much more relaxed than Saturday had been. After a "Goot" country breakfast, Kryss sat on the bed reading the newspaper, her legs wide apart, and I sat on the floor with my back against the bed watching a John Ford triple bill on TNT. If I even looked at her amorously, she growled.

About six o'clock we started making motions to get me to the train. We drove in silence up through Smyrna and past the statue of Baal next to Tranquility Travel. Kryss had told me it was the actual statue used in D.W. Griffith's *Intolerance* and a couple of other Hollywood films which came east as a promotion for some film and ended up as a curiosity at the travel agency.

Ten feet tall, it was a grim-looking grey and black figure that squatted down, holding a black snake that stared out from beneath a curly Sumerian haircut and a double set of horns. I waved hello as I usually did, but he never waved back. I guess movie stars are like that.

We got to Wilmington with no time for a long goodbye, which was just as well. "I have to take some of the girls to an audition in Philadelphia tomorrow, so I'll be late getting home," she said.

"I'll call Tuesday, then."

"Don't lose this new energy," she said with a slight smile. "It suits you better."

"I'll try not to." I stood like John Wayne in the last scene in *The Searchers*, right elbow held by my left hand. I felt almost as empty, too.

Except … except I felt angry all of a sudden, but not at Tom. "In fact," I said, "I think the energy level is on the rise."

"For God's sake, no!" she said as she turned to head back out to her car. "The world isn't ready for that."

From the escalator, I watched her walk stiff-legged out of the terminal's waiting room. Damn sexy pixie!

Chapter Eight

I had planned to share my return to the Renaissance faire world with Tom and Jill. There was the sense in the last couple of faires that I had done that I was sort of doing the show with them as my biggest boosters and supporters. The Company of the Silver Swan had almost been my "private" audience with Tom and Jill as the cheerleaders. I was so looking forward to a high five from him at the end of the season that, looking ahead at two months of rehearsals and seven weekends of show without him out there somewhere watching left me feeling especially empty.

I really did consider just walking away from it, even after Jill encouraged me to go on but my time with Krystal made me reconsider. I thought about him sitting on some cloud somewhere or in a hero's ale hall looking down on me and decided to give him a hell of a show.

Thus. it was with "the show must go on" running through my head that the Monday after Tom's funeral and my trip to Delaware, I was sitting in the producer's office on Fifth Avenue getting ready to work.

It was tough. Real tough.

The Artistic Director, Richard (The Dick) Mueller, was a commanding tower of Jell-O who hated rennies, patrons, actors in general and most of all, I think, himself for picking a career among them. He was a fortyish heroin addict, thin yet somehow flabby (an achievement) and perpetually working on a hangover.

"Are you going to be able to keep on with everything?" he asked.

I nodded and smiled with no humor. "I'll get it done, Richard," I said. "But thanks for caring."

"Sorry to hear about your friend," Dawn Faith, the co-producer of the faire said. Her tone was warm and sincere, her dark hazel eyes dilated and, as usual, she was high as a kite on coke.

"Yes," her husband Barry said more brusquely and with equally false sincerity. "If there's anything we can do …" He was the same producer who had stopped the fight master from bringing a stretcher onto the joust field two years previously. He wanted an actor who'd broken an ankle in a chuck hole to finish the scene and walk off. "Can't let the bad publicity affect the show" was his motto.

"Thanks, guys," I said as equally insincere, "but the best thing I can do is just jump right back into it." They both looked relieved.

"Red" and I exchanged a look; we both knew what Dawn and Barry were thinking, "Great, now we can work him harder for less money." Red smiled her wickedest smile and quickly hid it by shuffling through a stack of papers.

"Good, we can give you plenty to do!" Barry smiled at me, his best fatherly smile, like a father lizard.

"Where are we on the fights?"

I launched into a ten-minute summary of what I had done so far (which, with the crew I had, was a lot) and what I intended to do next. I outlined my plans for the joust as well as the schedule to exercise the horses, Whisky and Crusader. I gave them a list of the new weapons I would need, the places to buy them and cost estimates. I asked for thirty percent more than I needed so they had room to argue me down.

Dawn and Barry seemed a little stunned by so complete a report. It was a tactic I learned from Steve Manely, the choreographer I'd worked under during my first years at the fair; "Don't give'm a chance to question," he'd told me. The man was a genius.

I got a promise of the weapons I needed and nodded to Red.

"I need to talk to you about the *As You Like It* props," Red jumped in to say, diverting the three of them while they were still focused on my list of needed items. As they turned to look at Red, I made a mumbled goodbye and slipped out of the room with a grateful wink to Red. Anyone who's ever worked for the Faiths does it best from a distance.

Once out of the office, I engaged in the actor's religious ritual of calling my answering service from a pay phone. There was one message from a student canceling for Monday night's class and a call from Mandy telling me she hadn't gone into work. I called her back.

"Hi, it's Eric, how's Jill?"

"Irish in the extreme," Mandy said with a sly tone in her voice. "Robin had another fight with Dan and came over with little Danny. That cheered Jill up, but mostly she's allowing her anger to supersede her grief, and it's good for her."

"I'll be over late after my class tonight, I may have some fuel for that anger."

"What does that mean?"

"I just can't accept that Tom would choose to leave Jill, so I can't imagine it could have been suicide. Can you?"

"No, I've never known anyone as devoted as he is ... was ... to Jill."

"And can you imagine him to be so clumsy as to fall out a window even if he was having an asthma attack?"

Her pause was considered, and I could imagine her glasses slipping down her nose when she scrunched up her forehead. "No."

"That leaves only one explanation in my book; somebody helped him out that window."

"Fuck," Mandy said. I don't think I'd ever heard her so much as say "darn" all the time I'd known her so I know she believed it was possible. "What kind of proof do you have?" Her calm tone almost cracked as she asked me.

"None," I said as quietly as the garbage truck that was idling at the light would let me. "None so far anyway, but A.C.'s got somebody working on it for me. I may know something by tonight."

"Don't say anything to Jill, until you know something for sure."

"Yeah, I know, I've already been told I'm crazy."

"No argument there." She giggled.

"Thanks a lot for your confidence," I said with an answering laugh, "but really, how's she doing?"

"There were a lot of people at Tom's funeral who offered love and support. It's helped as best it could. But, as I said, she's angry at the universe."

"Well, hopefully we can do something to give her a specific focus for that anger if what I'm thinking works out."

"Take care, Eric," she said with a tone that felt like a hug. "I don't want you to become what the news calls 'collateral damage.'"

"See ya later." I quickly and hung up. *Collateral damage, my ass.* I'd been ground zero with Tom but, just like the Amazing Colossal Man, I'd survived. Only in my case, the pain was what was growing and mutating. Would it become a monster or a force for the good of mankind? Damned if I knew. I just knew I didn't want to end up on Boulder Dam with some B-actor stabbing me with a hypo!

With that thought buzzing in my brain, I hopped the train downtown to the candy store a couple of blocks from where Tom had worked.

Since my default view of the world was Monogram and Republic movies, it seemed that before I could go any further in the "someone actually defenestrated my friend" path, I had to go for the film noir default villain. I needed to talk to Tom's bookie.

His name was "Vinnie" and he was pretty much what you'd expect for a guy who sat behind the counter of a "candy store" all day with a cordless phone attached to his ear. He looked fiftyish, balding, as pallid as a dead fish and with a six-pack of rolls around his middle that made me wonder how he slid behind the counter.

"What can I do for you?" he asked as I strode through the door of the shop headed toward the back of the long, narrow candy store. There was a gorilla standing just inside the door reading a Baby Huey comic and sucking on a lollipop. Racks of outdated magazines slowed my progress.

"I came to ask questions about a former 'client' of yours." The glass counter that separated us contained a collection of plastic toys that had been current when I was a kid.

"This ain't an information counter. We sell soda and magazines and lotto tickets." He gave a subtle sign to the Monkeyboy at the front of the store, who obviously functioned as his security. Still seated in his swivel chair, he turned his back to me to go back to reading the racing form.

"It's Tom De Dannin," I said quickly before the door thug actually got his hands on me. "He took a brodie off a building last week, and I came to square things so there'll be no pressure on his wife." It wasn't really why I was there, but I didn't want to fight the Monkeyboy in leather who was lumbering toward me.

It worked.

Vinnie swiveled to face me. The Monkeyboy went back to his roost by the front to finish his comic book. I'll bet he moved his lips when he read.

"We don't do things that way." Vinnie said, "Family is free and clear of this stuff." Vinnie swung around and leaned on the glass case to look up at me with a philosophical expression. "Maybe some of those Dominicans do, or the young guys out of Elizabeth, but I don't. De Dannin. Long black hair, skinny, wears the little black hat?"

"Yeah." I wasn't feeling very tough; these guys were way out of my white-bread league but I sucked it up and tried to use my actor self and pretend I was playing one of the thugs I was always cast as.

"Good guy," Vinnie said, crossing himself. "Sorry to hear it, but he hasn't owed for two, three months now. Still comes by to pick up his lotto ticket, but he's jake with bets. He was losing heavy there for a while, but he got it together; kind of guy I like to do business with. Sorry to hear it."

"Nothing?" I asked, my tough guy mask falling away. My voice must have gone up two octaves. "He owes nothing?"

"Nope." He seemed to consider for a moment, then asked, "How?"

"We're not sure," I said honestly. "It could have been an accident or...." I shrugged.

"Hmm, too bad," Vinnie said. "He seemed like a nice guy, real regular Joe." He swiveled away from me again to go back to his racing form and the audience was over.

I nodded. I considered getting a lotto ticket but decided I'd probably used up all my luck for quite a while.

I walked out of the store into the hustle of the sidewalk, and I felt as if I'd stepped forward in time. I stood blinking in the bright sunlight for few minutes and then started to walk uptown slowly while I tried to make sense of it all.

If Tom did have a beef of some kind with this guy, it would be a long, hard end run to get around the wall of connections that Vinnie had. The store was barely a pretense of a real business. Yet my gut said that Vinnie had been straight, but what the hell did I know about this sort of thing? Tom was the closest I'd been to a mob-connected individual. It made me feel how protected my life had been from the dark corners of society.

I knew some tough customers, but they were marital artists and biker types—pretty much the kind of guy that, if they had a beef with you, walked up to you and cold cocked you to let you know it. Maybe A.C.'s guy Poppo could put out some feelers. Until then I was stymied.

Geez! I wish the Hardy Boys were backing me up!

Most people think of western swordplay in terms of some dandified, limp-wristed fencing match, calf-length white pants and a judge to rule on "right of way." Sort of, "Anyone for tennis" with skewers. Well, competition fencing is, but it was once a martial art as violent, vicious, and complete as any karate or kung fu style. That's the way I teach it as stunt combat. Anyone watching one of my classes might get a little flashback to the Musketeers' training hall.

Except we laugh a lot, and nobody really gets hurt.

On Monday night, I worked the six students pretty hard, and even though a teacher's not supposed to work as hard as his charges, I was pleasantly exhausted at ten o'clock when I ended the class at A.C.'s school. Smitty hadn't come in that night, so Vita was acting as my assistant. She collected the money while I put away the swords. Everyone else had already left.

"I really liked that leg-trip-kill-thing," Vita said. She locked the cabinet where I kept my weapons.

"I stole that from Tom, and he got it from a Jackie Chan flick."

"I should have known, either Bill Hobbs or Jackie."

"I do come up with original ideas," I asserted as I stripped out of my workout clothes. Vita started to do the same. Even if we didn't have ancient history as lovers, the life of an actor tends to destroy any illusions of modesty, especially the communal world of Ren faire actors.

"I don't know about that," A.C. said as he entered. Then he stopped short when he saw our state of undress.

"Hi!" Vita, clad in bra and panties, said cheerfully. She sat down to pull on her pants. A.C. stood there, not sure where to look, trying not to stare at Vita.

"I love to watch a black man blush," I said with a gleeful laugh.

"And I," he said in the sinister tone which had gotten him so much work as a thug, "love to see tall white men bruise." He added a little "he-he-he" that was straight out of a Peter Lorre movie.

He finally opted to go into his office, and I followed. "What did Poppo say?" I asked. He looked at me oddly.

"Well, on that guy Vinnie you talked to," he said as he pulled a thick folder of papers out of his desk, "he said the guy's got some powerful connections, but a straight-up reputation; he doesn't have a rep for strong arm stuff."

"That was my feeling," I said," but what do I know?"

He still looked at me with a strange expression. "You sure you can handle this?" He held up the thick Manila envelope. "Poppo Xeroxed these; they're pretty graphic. "

I took a deep breath. "I don't have a choice," I said. "I see his face every time I close my eyes anyway." It was still a painful shock when I opened the folder. It was graphic in the extreme with Xeroxed photos of Tom's body from every angle, a diagram of his position in relation to the building, a photo of the landing window the police had decided he'd fallen from, a coroner's report and the autopsy photos.

The autopsy photos were the worst. I felt my bile rising and actually had to steady myself by grabbing the back of a chair. I forced myself to read the whole report.

"Earth to Eric," A.C. broke into my train of thought. "You okay?" I realized that Vita was standing beside him. I must have been absorbed in the report a good ten minutes.

"Sorry, guys."

"Don't worry," A.C. said. "Let's go downstairs for a slice and a soda and talk."

However ghoulish the pictures were, they didn't stop me from absorbing three slices of pizza.

"Nowhere in that report does it say anything about a beret pin." Vita said, "and it says a beat cop was on the scene within three to five minutes."

"It also says nobody actually saw him fall," I added. "A woman on the third floor heard Tom hit and looked out. She sent her neighbor down and immediately called 911. I'd say the body was only alone a minute or two."

"That could be enough time for some kid—"

"This is Bayridge we're talking about," I insisted, "not Red Hook, and it was a closed courtyard."

"Granted," A.C. said, "but it could have been ripped off. You have to admit it."

I did not want to lose the focus point for my grief and anger, but I had to be logical even if I was half-Irish/Scot. I nodded. "Yeah, it's possible."

A.C. looked at me hard for a moment and then nodded. "Okay, that's understood," he spoke with such quiet intensity that I became a little frightened, "Look at this."

A.C. flipped to one of the photos of Tom on the coroner's table. It was a left profile, head and shoulders. Clearly visible on his temple was a faint bruise the size of a nickel. Vita and I stared at it.

"That's the exact spot on the temple you strike for a knockout blow with a dan bong." A.C. said. A dan bong is a little hardwood stick, not much longer than a ballpoint pen, that Hwa Rang Do stylists use to attack nerve centers. Other styles call similar weapons kongas or kubotans or yawara sticks.

"You're saying you think he was murdered, too?"

"It is possible that that bruise in that exact spot is coincidental from the fall, but I doubt it." A.C. nodded. "I think it's highly likely that was a deliberate strike." He tapped the photo with a knuckle. "It's how I'd do it."

We both stared at him, dumbfounded. He had the real-world fight experience; he had done some time as a bounty hunter and worked with a cousin doing black ops for the DEA. He didn't joke about stuff like that.

"Tom was a tough fuck," A.C. said in the same serious tone. "If I had to disable him, I'd do it by surprise." He flicked his hand up and flicked me quickly on the left temple with a pencil I hadn't seen in his hand.

"Ow!" I squealed and jumped back. "That hurt."

"See, even if I'm talking to you and with your reflexes, I make a slightly exaggerated gesture with my hand, and bam!"

"If he didn't block it, or even partly blocked it," I said, "it would stun him enough...." I couldn't finish. I felt sick to my stomach again.

"Enough," A.C. said. "Especially if there were two of them. He wasn't a big man. Two guys could easily heave him out the window."

"Shit!" I hissed. I had to sit down on one of the folding chairs.

The three of us sat thinking for a while, saying nothing, each lost in the image of that smirking face we knew in the moments before he went out that window and then as he was on that autopsy table.

Vita finally broke the silence with all we were thinking. "What now?"

A.C. and I just stared at each other for a long moment. I felt a strange pull in my gut, down deep inside—a cold spot that grew from a pinpoint to fill me. In a voice oddly free of emotion, I said, "We find the sons of bitches that killed Tom, and we make them pay."

They both nodded.

The moment passed, and I felt a surge of doubt as Vita asked, "How?"

"We start with questions," A.C. said. "Tom's neighborhood. Look for anyone who saw anything—"

"But the police," Vita injected.

"They have a vested interest in closing out case files," A.C. finished. "Our job is to keep the case going."

"This might help," I said, reaching into my ever-present side pack. I pulled out a sketchbook. I spent my time after I met with Vinnie doing these," I said proudly. I produced two drawings I'd made during the day: one, a profile, full figure head and shoulders of "Blondie" and one a considerably less detailed attempt at Mr. Gunns.

"Holy shit," Vita said with her usual subtlety, "these are great." A.C. examined them for a few seconds, reading aloud the height, weight and other details I had scribbled in the side margins of the drawings.

"How good are these?" he asked.

"I did a lot of meditation and visual recall work," I answered. "They are as dead-on as they can be."

He nodded. "And these?" He pointed to the patches I had indicated on Blondie's long coat.

"They looked like merit patches," I said. "Like you'd get in Boy Scouts, but with, like, city and country names."

"Uh-huh," he said noncommittally. He continued to stare at my drawing of Blondie. "And these?" He pointed. "On the upper chest — are they pins?"

"Yeah," I said. "Pins and competition buttons and —" I suddenly choked as I looked at the drawings and remembered Blondie's arrogant walk outside the electronics store on Canal Street. And I also remembered the plain black beret on Tom De Dannin's head. "Oh my God," I whispered.

"In Viet Nam," A.C. said, barely audible, "they used to take ears to confirm a kill."

———

My ride into Brooklyn passed as a blur. All the suppositions and possibilities whirling around in my head kept coming back to the same thing: Tom was dead and I was not. That meant I had an inherent duty to find out the whys and who's. And it didn't come down to the greater good, the moral right or the just and vengeful thing to do. I would find out because if I'd been the one lying in a courtyard in Brooklyn with my head split open and Tom was alive, he would've found out who had done it and made them pay.

We were a family with ties in heart and soul that were deeper than blood. From the moment we'd met, we'd each known without a word or gesture, each would "take the blade" for the other. Every warrior has recognized a brother in arms since the dawn of time. Whether racial memory, past life recall, or fantasy spawned of too many Stewart Granger films, it made no difference. We both knew. Jill knew too, and was both in awe of it as well as matter-of-factly accepting. I've only known that mutual absolute certainty four times in my life, with four entirely different people: A.C., Krystal, a lesbian named Sheila from Canada and Tom.

Now some son of a bitch had cut down my comrade in dreams.

My brother.

It was just past midnight when I left the train at Kings Highway, walked the three blocks to Albermarle Road and ran the four flights to Mandy and Don's apartment, forming something of a game plan. I paused to take a deep breath before knocking on the door.

"Just watch my back for me, Tom," I whispered as I knocked. "And do a better job than I did for you."

Don opened the door. He wore a Victorian smoking jacket and held a brandy snifter filled with ginger ale. "Hi, Eric," he said smoothly. "Jill and Mandy are in Jill's room."

Mandy's workroom had become Jill's sanctum sanctorum since she'd come to stay. Lots of pillows, pictures of Tom and a box of tissues by the futon. Mandy's soft sculptured doll-making supplies, bolts of cloth and Mandy's booth banner from the Ren faire lined the walls of the small room, making it feel like a sheik's storage tent.

Mandy and Jillian were seated on the futon looking through photo albums. "This was the first Balticon masquerade Tom got me to compete in," Jill was saying when I walked in. "He got me liquored up. I not only wasn't nervous, I enjoyed strutting around on stage as Grania O'Malley. He had to pull me off when our presentation was done. I didn't want to go." She had a faraway, bittersweet look in her eyes. Mandy watched her and listened with a warm smile fixed on her face. She'd heard each story half a dozen times, but it didn't matter. Jill needed to say all the words again.

"Hey, guys," I said cheerfully. "How's tricks?"

"Eric!" Jill noticeably brightened and started to rise, but I crouched beside her for her hug. No need for her to expend energy.

"Sorry I'm so late. How ya doin'?" I asked.

I caught Mandy's eye over Jill's shoulder. She nodded a "she's doing better" look.

"Mandy's been an angel," Jill said, "letting me go on about Tom. She's heard all those stories so many times."

Jill didn't see Mandy's almost embarrassed look, but I did and enjoyed it. She didn't take compliments well, her self-effacement was her personal armor against the world.

"How was your weekend with Krystal?" Jill asked. She and Tom had met Kryss after a *Peter Pan* performance in Virginia when they'd driven over after a SheVa con.

"Exhausting," I said with a chagrined smirk. Mandy and Jill both laughed. Jill hugged me tighter.

I took her by the shoulder and held her away for a closer look. "Really though, how are you doin'?"

"I'm really as all right as I can be," Jill said emphatically. "Don't worry so about me. You sound like—" She stopped herself with a choked sound before she said "Tom."

It made me all the more determined to tell them what I'd learned. Jill was strong enough to hear it. Ultimately, it was she who would have final approval of any actions we took. Don came in with a snifter of ginger ale for me, and we all sat in a little huddle for a while exchanging pleasantries.

When I dropped my information bomb, they were as stunned as I had been by the discovery. Jillian took it better than I could have hoped, her grief converting instantly to a focused anger that was as bloody Irish as revolution. When she looked at my drawings of Blondie and Mr. Gunns, I was reminded of that same fire that had often burned in Tom's eyes.

"Where do we go from here?" I asked when I had finished my tale. "I have some ideas, but—"

"Elementary, my dear Holmes," Don said. "We investigate." He smiled tentatively to lighten the mood.

Mandy rose to the bait. "We can't make bricks without straw!" Jill and I looked into each other's eyes. That quiet fire inside her communicated directly to me, erasing any lingering doubts I had.

For the next half hour we plotted and planned our counter attack. Then, Don copied my drawings and scanned them into Mandy's computer. Jill printed across the top: "Wanted for questioning in the death of Thomas De Dannin." She added my service number and name to the bottom. We decided against adding a reward on the first batch. Mandy was supportive of all of us, quietly reassuring, commenting, giving neck rubs, and offering tea. Soon we had fifty "Wanted" posters for each guy.

"I'll run off a bunch more at work," Mandy said, "and Jill and Don and I can put them up in Jill's neighborhood. A lot of street people knew Tom and respected him. Somebody will know something."

"And they'll talk to us where they wouldn't talk to the police," Jill added.

"I'll put some up in the neighborhood of Tom's job to cover all our bases," I said.

We all felt like we'd at least taken action after the limbo of the last week and we felt, I think, righteously exhausted from it.

We said our goodnights, and Jill asked me to stay with her again. We settled under the sheets with her arms wrapped around me. Jillian sighed, grabbing tight around my chest.

"Tom fought a duel for me once, did I tell you that, Eric?"

"A long time ago, hon."

"It was when we were living in Baltimore. He wasn't my 'boyfriend' yet. We'd just flirted at Medieval Society events and I mean, he was this kid, you know. I was a mature twenty-two and he was only eighteen. There was this other guy, a needle dick, giant auxiliary policeman whose Medieval Society name was Grey Fork, who thought he was God's gift to women. He came onto me real strong one evening at a medieval party at a college hall. Tom saw and called him a cad. Can you imagine that word coming out of Tom's mouth?"

"I can just barely," I said with a chuckle, "Although hairbag would have been his choice."

"He made cad sound that bad. So Grey Fork called him something and then challenged him, figuring Tom would back down. Grey Fork was your size and Tom was even scrawnier then. Tom called him on it: "Swords, here and now!" and somebody handed them two epees and wham! Without masks or marshals they went at it over couches, into walls. Grey Fork was good, but Tom was magnificent! He took every button off Grey Fork's tunic before he disarmed him and made him apologize to me and swear never to speak to me again. That's the night I fell in love with him."

She snuggled her cheek against my chest. After a while she said, "I can deal with it better thinking somebody killed him, that he didn't leave me willingly, you know, even if we don't get them. Good night, Eric."

"Me too, Jill. Good night."

Chapter Nine

Everyone started early the next day, the "Wanted" poster having filled all of us with a new sense of purpose. Don had some free time, so he and Jill walked her neighborhood putting up posters. They met Lily for lunch. Don went off to work and Lily took over staying with Jill. They put up over a hundred posters by the end of the day. It exhausted Jill, but it was just what she needed.

I was off early to rehearsal upstate at the faire site, a former private golf course in New Jersey about forty minutes from Manhattan. Smitty picked me up at the bus stop.

"Hey, boss," he said, "want to stop for food or head straight up?" I climbed in his VW beetle, affectionately named the Jugglebug, and stowed my side pack in the back.

"Is Kelly up at the site yet?"

"He showed up just as I finished feeding the horses."

"Then let's head to the faire."

It was only a ten-minute trip to the little world that was the Great Eastern Renaissance Faire that was nestled between two low hills. It was a seventeen-acre complex that was the gateway to another world for upwards of a hundred thousand people in any given season.

Ten acres of graveled and rutted fields were set aside for patron parking, and six acres were a palisade-enclosed, Tudor-style village. Inside were vendor stalls, performing stages and a tourney field where we would be jousting and holding the human chess game. A small lake (or large pond depending on whether you were an optimist or a pessimist) bordered the western edge of the village. We all just called it the Sink Hole, though it had a name on the map.

Smitty drove us around the back where the administration building/costume shop and barn were located and we met up with Kelly Stevens, my joust partner. He had already saddled both horses and was waiting for me.

"Hey, Eric," Kelly said. "Let's ride." Kelly spit—did I mention he chewed tobacco incessantly? Carlos, who worked the stable during most of the year with Smitty, stood near the stable door and waved when I stepped out of the car. I mounted Whisky, and Kelly took Crusader. It felt good to be on the old "warhorses" after the semi-trained horses we had ridden for the Cloisters. We spent the afternoon riding patterns in and around the joust field to get a sense of where we were with them, though both horses seemed to be readier to go than we were.

Horses see things bigger than they are, so a fence or a man looks pretty scary to them. It takes a tremendous amount of patient training to get a horse to jump an obstacle. It takes infinitely more to get them to charge at another horse. Whiskey and Crusader had gotten to the point where they loved it and half our efforts at any show were trying to curb their enthusiasm when we made the turn and they saw each other.

Smitty had been exercising them regularly for weeks to get off their winter fat. Both were in fine shape. The day was set aside for them to get used to us again as much as the other way around.

"I've been thinking about the body hit," Kelly said as we rode through the faux village. "I think this is the year we gotta do it." He forced the words around a particularly huge plug of tobacco. "Them guys in Texas and Michigan are already doing it."

It was a big issue on the faire circuit. Body hit or not to body hit—or as I liked to think of it, "Are you feeling lucky, ren punk?"

Modern jousting is dangerous enough with man, horse and Murphy's Law dancing around on the field at the same time. We choreograph the action, wear pads, use breakaway lances of balsa and pine and traditionally take the impact of the lance on the shield we carry for the safest possible outcome. In the last couple of years, however, some adrenaline junky riders had begun to take the impact on their chest armor in the mistaken belief that it was more period accurate.

It isn't.

No one in their right mind ever took a real lance strike on their chest when a shield was available; in fact, they had built jousting armor with a built-in extra shield, but the precedent had been set in the movies and other Renaissance faires. We had to play to audience perceptions as much or more than to historical accuracy. We are, after all, part thrill show.

"I've been thinking about it, too," I said. Then I laughed a grim laugh. "I even discussed it with my buddy Tom, who thought I was absolutely crazy but who wanted to do it himself."

I started off down Hawkers Lane, one of the two streets that ran through the village. Most of the stalls, booths, and Tudor-style buildings were still winterized and boarded up, though some merchants (who owned the buildings but leased the land) had already slapped a new coat of whitewash on them and re-caulked roofs.

One of the refits was a grog shop, newly named "The Fresh Coffin," with a sign hanging out front that showed a knight lying in a fresh coffin with a sword through him.

We both caught sight of it at the same time. "Good thing I don't believe in omens," Kelly said after a pause.

"Me neither," I said, "Since I'll be taking the body hit!"

Kelly spit and said, "Uhuh!"

Damn eloquent for a cowboy.

Kelly and I rode until dusk, after which I hustled back to the city to take a class with A.C. He rewarded my zeal by trying to beat me to death along with a few other hardy souls who were searching for martial perfection.

"You need to stretch more," A.C. said after class. "For some reason you're real tense." He had a snide smirk on his lips and I tried not to take him too seriously. It had been a good, hard class that had driven away a few demons, at least temporarily and I was pleasantly exhausted.

"I just might be tense 'cause I'm worried that I have a psychotic instructor."

"What else is new?" he smirked.

"Well," I said, "since you asked," and launched into an account of the skull session at Mandy's.

"Good plan," he said as he removed his dobuk top. "I'm seeing Poppo tomorrow, and I'll pass the mug drawing along to him. He may be able to get access to that new state/federal computer hook-up that runs photos high speed to match it with Identi-kit drawings, but the drawings might not have enough detail for the computers."

"Truth be told," I said, "I never got a real clear look at either man's facial features; that's why I had so much detail on Blondie's jacket. Between the glasses and hair—"

"Don't backpedal," he said to me. "Your descriptions were pretty detailed and that might be enough with the new protocols the federal system has."

"Sounds like technology to me," I said, stripping out of my own workout clothes. "I'm a pre-firearms type."

"I'll handle the tech stuff," he said, taking off his kick pants to reveal his running shorts underwear. "You just grunt and hit the bad guys with sticks."

As long as I've known A.C., I still don't know his first name or why he always wore running shorts instead of underwear. My curiosity finally got the better of me, so I decided to risk a follow-up beating to supplement my bruises from class. "Why the hell don't you wear normal underwear?" I asked. There was a moment where he gave me a steely stare and I was pretty sure asking his name would get me killed.

Finally A.C. laughed. "College," he said as if it were explanation enough. When I just stared back at him he elaborated. "Being a football star, I was often 'taken out' after games by well-off, white, suburban gridiron groupies of the female persuasion."

"So?"

"So, in the event a husband came home unexpectedly, and I had to bolt out the back door in a hurry...."

"A black guy running in a white suburb in the Eighties had better have been in jogging shorts," I finished for him.

His grin was positively diabolical. "Fortunately," he added, "the occasion arose only once. Seems that my coach had a stricter curfew than the suburban husbands."

I had to ask.

———

Being the non-drinking son of an alcoholic has its drawbacks in moments of extreme depression. For me to take a drink would be damn close to putting a gun to my head, so I have substitutes for my addictive tendencies—some good, some bad. None as bad as booze.

Women are a two-edged sword in that department, seeing as how they can choose to *not* be addicted back, and the ones who do choose to be, if "choose" is the right word, are often more screwed up than I am. My contact with the fair sex had become more constructive as time had gone on. I lucked out big time with Kryss.

Exercise—martial arts and staged fighting included—had been a real plus to beat the blues in the last couple of years, and that is truly evolutionary. I was a sickly child so the day I discovered the sword was a magical one, with the sword almost my magic wand that inspired me to work past my lung issues. Every day that I was able to run up a flight of stairs without wheezing was a victory for me.

My one constant addiction, and one I acquired quite young, was like a churned and frozen dream. Ice cream.

I'll even take ice cream over anything but honest-to-gosh hot-monkey love (really, an old girlfriend called it that). Breyer's vanilla fudge twirl. All-natural ingredients: pure sugar, cream, vanilla bean, cocoa. Heaven! Add some chopped up bananas for the potassium rush and voila! The ultimate hurt/comfort food.

I ate a lot of ice cream and bananas the first five weeks after Tom's death, ran two to three miles a day, took a lot of hard classes with A.C. pushing me to exhaustion, and often cried myself to sleep. The hot-monkey part just didn't seem to fit the scheme of things after the memorial love-making with Jillian and the ash hauling with Krystal in Delaware.

And of course, I choreographed a hell of a lot of chess game fights for the Ren faire. Twelve kick-ass fights with everything from quarterstaves to the farmer's scythe we nicknamed "the weed whacker." It really was the best work I'd ever done, with every trick that Tom had ever pulled on me made more theatrical and out there for the public to see for seven weekends through the summer.

It became my monument to Tom. All my performers either sensed or knew the importance this work had for me. Some, like Smitty and Vita, had known Tom but it seemed like all of the performers put their guts into the show as well.

By the time opening day arrived I knew we would give the customers the best Ren faire experience they would ever have. My only regret was that I wouldn't have Tom at the cast party at the end of the season telling how I'd done this or that historically inaccurately while he patted me on the back and said, "Great show, Highpockets!"

That month and change was uneventful after we put out the flyers, falling into a pattern that could almost be called normal. Most nights I stayed at Mandy and Don's, sleeping with Jillian as sort of her teddy bear/bed warmer, although our intimacy of the first night was never repeated, nor even mentioned.

We spoke often of her life with Tom, of the people he'd helped and lives he'd touched. We also spoke of the progress on the coming Faire. Robin often arrived with little Danny (usually to avoid a screaming match with big Dan over some new Irish charmer she was seeing) and the kid was a great source of joy and distraction.

Jill was also taking an active hand in helping Mandy prepare her stock of soft sculpture puppets for opening day of the faire. It was a fact we all found encouraging.

I brought some drawing gear and many nights, when I wasn't involved in rehearsals, we'd sit around the living room, Mandy and Jill stuffing and sewing little grotesque heads, Don doing layouts for a job or reading, and me doing some pen and ink drawings for a fanzine or small press publisher. Robin stopped by less frequently and when she did she regaled us with tales of her new boyfriend. It was clear she was floating on the cloud of new love. We had a little worry that she was rebounding, but it was so nice to see her beaming that we just smiled and enjoyed her delight by proxy.

I worked twice on *Guiding Light* as an extra cop, once on *Another World* as a stuntman doing a bar fight. I spoke to Krystal frequently, but her teaching schedule and my show work didn't allow for any visits.

Oddly, those weeks were some of the most pleasant ones I can recall. The sense of community and camaraderie made me feel protected. It was only in the deep of the night with Jill sobbing herself to sleep in my arms that it all came into perspective.

In my "spare" time I continued with the poster campaign, going to Tom's job, the restaurant where I'd seen Mr. Gunns, and even to the area of the blind alley, talking to anyone who would listen. No one recalled anything.

Then, in mid-July on a hot, rainy Tuesday about a week before the Faire was to open, I got a message on my service from a "Mr. Smith" regarding the De Dannin matter.

"If you would like to find out what really happened to Mister De Dannin call this number at exactly six o'clock sharp." The voice on the recording sounded flat. Not unaccented, just flat. The background was just noisy street sounds. He left a 718 number and then the line cut off.

I was at the offices of the Ren faire doing some rehearsal space rental reports and I used the landline from Red's office. I was nervous as heck; it was the first response we had gotten from any of the posters, so I had no idea what to expect.

I played the message several times and just stared at the receiver. It was only four thirty. I made myself concentrate on the paperwork, but I had to redo several pages because I kept looking up at the clock.

Finally, at exactly six, I made the call.

"You left a message for me about Thomas De Dannin?" I said when the phone went live.

"Who am I talkin' to?" the voice on the phone said. It was flat, and oddly accented, like someone was trying to do a Brooklyn accent. In the background I could hear street noise again—it had to be a payphone.

"My name's Eric Knight, like it says on the flyer. What do I call you?"

"Uh … Deep Throat will do." A little chuckle. A slip into something not Brooklyn, but what?

"What do you know?" I asked.

"What is your interest in De Dannin?" he asked me.

"He was my friend," I said. "Do you have something to tell me or not?" I was so on edge from having to wait for the call that I was getting annoyed with the double-talk from that strange voice.

"What kinda dough are you payin'?"

"For what?" I asked.

Did he actually say dough? Who talks like that? What the hell kind of old movie did this jerk step out of?

"For the dope on who killed your friend."

That stunned me. Here was somebody who said it: "killed your friend." Our poster had said simply "Information about the death of Thomas De Dannin." It said nothing about how he died. Nothing about him being killed.

"You still there, buddy?" the flat voice said.

"Yeah," I said, "I'm still here." I kept trying to place the accent of the voice. It was odd; somehow, I had heard it before, but I just couldn't place it.

Then it hit me. I'd heard that flat, atonal American speech before, years ago. It was Lawrence Oliver's version of standard American.

Shit, I thought. But I said, "I don't pay until I see a face, and then only when I have proof. For proof, I'll pay plenty." *God, now I'm talking old Warner Brothers dialogue.*

"Okay," said Deep Throat. "Bring cash to the roof he 'fell' from. Seven o'clock tonight—alone."

"I'm in Astoria."

"So?"

Hmm … he doesn't know the city. Any idiot knows it's more than an hour even if there are no train delays.

"I can't schedule the trains," I said aloud, slurring the "Sch" to "Sh" like the English do. "I can't be there before eight or nine."

"Schedule your bum out there at nine." The son of a bitch fell for it and slipped back to his natural voice that sounded like "Shed dual."

A click followed by a dial tone. I just stared at the receiver again like it was a trained snake that I expected to jump out and bite me.

"Holy crap!" I said out loud.

I waited just long enough to draw a breath, then dialed A.C.'s voicemail. I knew he had a job that day, but I called his school after the voicemail anyway and repeated my story to the answering machine. Then I called Mandy's apartment. She would be home from the Army base by then.

Jill and Mandy got on the two extensions. I had to calm myself down and speak slowly when I filled them in.

"You can't go alone," Mandy said with horror in her voice. "We can—"

"No way," I said firmly. "You two are not coming. If anything physical happens, I want a big scary backup, preferably an African-American who is an excellent thug type. One named A.C."

"He's right," Jill said. It always amazes me how she can be so Irish and so logical at the same time. "We'd only get in the way, but what if you can't get a hold of A.C.?"

"I'll get somebody from the school or the Faire's fight corps. I promise I will not go alone."

"Okay, then," Mandy said back to her calm, even tone, "What can we do?"

"Well, I wanted to let you know and to run my guesses about 'Deep Throat' past Jill."

"You think he's Blondie?" Jill asked. "And that he's English."

"That's my guess."

"How do you come to that?" Mandy asked.

"Mr. Gunns had a slight, but real, Cork accent," Jill said. "Tom had a good ear."

"And I figure it's a small circle of villains;" I said, "It's hard to keep a secret otherwise."

"You really believe that, Eric?" Mandy said, "Or is it just a comfort thought for us?"

"It's a comfort thought for me," I said. "I'd like to think it's only two bastards, not all of 'T.H.R.U.S.H.'"

The city smelled like a wet dog by the time I got to Bay Ridge. The heat of the day hadn't let up at all and despite the drizzle, the humidity was still high. I hadn't been able to get hold of A.C., but I had Vita and her boyfriend Rick as my backup. It was eight thirty.

"You want us to come up with you?" Vita asked. Rick was a little over six foot and built like a linebacker. I didn't know much about him, save that he made Vita happy and liked to play *Dungeons & Dragons*. We all called him "The Hunk." I figured if worse came to worst, he could fall on any felons. Vita, I knew, could kick the stuffing out of almost anybody alive except me and A.C. and maybe Rick.

"No." I shook my head. "If it's a real tip, I don't want to scare the guy off."

"Not much we can do from down here," Rick said. He had a cultured, southern voice, very soft-spoken. "First we'd hear about trouble would be tomorrow's paper."

A "hunk" with a point.

"If I come down first," I said, ignoring his ominous statement, "follow the guy behind me. If he comes down first, I'll signal you from the roof." I produced a pen flashlight and clicked it on and off. Tom Swift and his Electric Crime Solver.

"Be careful," Vita said dramatically. I nodded with equal drama and headed off, swinging my umbrella with forced nonchalance as I hummed, "Do Not Forsake Me" from *High Noon*.

Entering the building felt eerie. The familiar sounds of TVs playing too loud and voices that echoed through the apartment building hallways were a little off kilter.

I felt a chill, a goosebump edginess that grew in intensity as I ascended the stairs. I avoided looking at Apartment 2B's door with great deliberation forcing my mind away from the last time I'd been in there packing up Jill and Tom's stuff.

The roof door stood ajar when I got to it. I paused to listen. From somewhere below I could hear Robert Stack's voice on *Unsolved Mysteries* and a reggae tune cranked too loud. From above, I heard nothing. I went up.

The door opened onto a roof, flat, holding a couple-of-antenna, our-chimneys, two wash-lines and some-lawn furniture and other assorted junk regular old roof.

It was shaped like a giant "E" on its side, the irregular face mirroring the exact twin across the courtyard. The roof door let me out where the center prong of the "E" joined the main body. Five steps ahead of me was the edge of the roof, from which I could look down on the spot where Tom had died. The thought of it made me a little queasy.

I heard a sound to my right, a scuff of shoes on the roof gravel.

I turned just in time to see an aluminum baseball bat coming straight at my face. Reflexes and fifteen years with a sword in my hand got my umbrella into a quarte parry and immediate backhand reply to my attacker's right temple. I jumped back in a parody *en garde*.

My assailant was not alone. From the other side of the stairwell door, a second figure emerged wielding a wooden Louisville slugger. He swung down at my head.

I lunged with my umbrella straight at his solar plexus and nailed him hard enough so that he dropped his bat.

Before I could follow up, Aluminum was at me again, swinging wildly. He drove me toward the roof's edge. I didn't look back, but I knew it was a bare pace behind me to oblivion.

Slugger hesitated to gather his wits about him and decide just how to pound me into Jello.

It was pretty clear to me that I had to finish this soon, or they'd have my butt in a basket and finish it for me.

I dropped into a low lunge, a sloppy passata sotto, my "point" hitting him square in the groin. Then I fell onto my left arm and swept his legs with Tom's trip move so that Slugger fell hard on his tailbone.

When he hit the gravel, I jumped on him with everything I had, kneeing his groin hard for good measure. I dropped my umbrella and yanked the bat from his hands with both of mine.

Everything was jumbled and yet moving in slow motion at the same time. My head turned up to look for Aluminum as he was at me again, his weapon raised to bash my brains in, so I swung the bat low and fast at his legs.

There was a satisfying crunch and a Latin curse as Aluminum went down. Slugger was underneath me still gasping for air and moaning from the groin hit. He made an *Ugh!* sound as I pushed off of him and staggered to my feet.

I didn't wait around to see if there were more of them. I ran straight through the open roof doorway and all the way down to where Vita and Rick waited on the street.

"That was quick," Vita said, in a tone that was a set up to a quip, but when she saw my agitated state she asked seriously, "What happened?"

I told them as we raced back up the stairs. I was wheezing like a geezer and sweating like a runner. I was also scared out of my mind but I was angry as well so I pushed on behind them, still carrying the bat.

The roof door was closed, which was funny, because I didn't remember closing it.

Rick pushed ahead, a buck knife miraculously in his hand.

"I'll go left," he whispered. I nodded. He pushed the door open and darted out with me a hair behind him. He dodged left, I went right.

There was no one hiding.

There was a gasp from Vita and I whirled. The two bat wielders were where I'd left them, but they were unmoving and strangely quiet. When I got closer, I saw why: both had nice, neat bullet holes in the middle of their foreheads.

Chapter Ten

"Gather round, good people!" the grand crier intoned, "and be presented to his royal majesty King Stephen!" The good King Stephen ascended the wooden steps to his greeting platform on the stockade wall with nary a wobble to betray his massive drinking bout the night before. James Allenrod, the actor portraying him, was a legend for his beer capacity, and unlike many legends there was much basis in fact for this one.

"Good people of England," he began, "we are pleased you could attend us here in our summer residence." He continued his five-minute greeting ritual, setting up the scenario for the waiting crowd and putting a plug in for the merchant of the day. I paid no attention to him; my eyes were on the crowd.

I was positioned behind the split wood palisade wall that ran around the perimeter of the fantasy English village that was the Great Eastern Renaissance Faire. It was ten fifty-five in the morning on the first Saturday of the Faire and the crowd outside was already in the hundreds. They had started arriving around nine, which always amused us performers since we didn't have to be at the costume shop to start suiting up until nine thirty.

Most of the performers had an odd love/hate relationship with the crowds who came to our shows. It was almost as if we were embarrassed that we liked the life so much—that we needed to set ourselves above the crowd so we wouldn't be considered "weird." I think many actors were afraid that if they weren't in the show, they would be in the crowds themselves because we were all just a little outside the twentieth-century model of normal.

Many of those people who arrived early wore their version of "period garb"—teens in jeans and sneakers with a homespun tabard thrown over a poet's shirt their girlfriends had lent them. Those guys came to impress upon their girls that they could be a real Romeo (and see some wenches at the same time). The girlfriends, high school girls in waist cinchers and low-cut peasant blouses came to act "deliciously slutty," to stare at the cute actors in tights and then go demurely home with their slob boyfriends. The families, usually with two and three kids in tow, the dad a little soft, the mom a little harried, came to show the children there was something besides video games that could be fun.

There were also the different ones, the Ren groupies who found the illusion of the Faire preferable to their weekly existence. They bought season tickets and rarely missed a day. They wore elaborate fantasy costumes and carried sharp steel swords that cost thousands of dollars. They belonged to various fantasy, medieval, or Renaissance recreation groups that met year-round, took persona names and affected anachronistic courtly manners.

Most of the actors were really scared of this last group, worried as only one who lives in a world bordered on all sides by unreality can be of people who blur the line between the real and the fantastic intentionally.

Tom was like them, and part of me was, too. I know if I hadn't found a way to make it a business, I might well have haunted the fringes as well because Tom had been right; the sword was my world and that meant so was the ren world. I knew many of these groupies by either their real or persona names, spoke to them (in character as the evil Sir Angus Burns), and counted some of them my friends. Like Tom.

I went from my crowd at the stockade wall to check along Hawker's Lane, the main merchant's road toward my first scene at the queen's dais. I waved hello to Mandy, Robin and Don who were putting the last touches on Mandy's hawking stand before the rush the first day.

Jill had decided to sit the first weekend out, and she and Lily had gone up to Boston to visit friends. Dear as Jill was and is to me, we all needed to be minding the show that weekend and not her, and she knew it. It would have been hard for her to wander the grounds without seeing her personal knight in shining black beret as well. It was just too soon. It might always be too soon.

"I'll come a little later in the season," she had said as Lily hustled them and their bags into the car service at the curb on Wednesday night. "Five days in Boston will do me wonders, and I'll be out from underfoot."

I could read her expression. She was about to add something like, "Tom used to always say I got underfoot when he was getting ready for a convention," but swallowed it. She had started to do that a lot. We could all see the unvoiced sentences whenever she spoke, but we never said anything to each other.

"Good, it should be ready for public viewing by week three." I smiled. She gave me a sympathy hug.

"It'll be fine," she said. "You're just being dramatic."

"The pot calling the kettle black, Madame Seaneche."

"Hurry up, guys," Lily called from across the seat where she was buried in some of Jill's bags," the meter is running."

"'Bye," Jill said as she leaned out the open car door to kiss me on the cheek. "You take care, Eric."

She studied me. "I had a disturbing dream last night," she added. "Nothing I could remember clearly when I awoke, except that I think it involved the Norns, the sisters who spun the thread of fate for men. I don't know what it means, but just be careful. I come from a long line of Irish witches."

"Aren't you all?" I smiled. I saw her expression darken and added, "I promise I'll be extra careful."

"And wear Courage," she added, a little insistently. I stared at her for a moment, a little stunned as she continued, "I … uh … Tom would have wanted you to." She waited until I responded to her strange request, despite Lily calling again from inside the car.

When Tom had proposed to Jill, he'd sworn that Courage would always be ready to protect her. When he married her, it had been on his hip.

No one had ever worn it but Tom. The importance of her asking me to wear it was great.

"Yes, I promised, every morning at King's Address." She smiled and finally let Lily drag her into the car.

So it was that Courage, its silver caged hilt wired into the scabbard, "peacebonded," so it couldn't be drawn, clattered at my hip as I walked down Hawkers Lane that first day of the faire.

"How's the crowd?" Mary Ann at the sachet booth called. She sold scented sachets and dried flower wreaths to the customers.

"They look like they need some good scents!" I called back.

"Aye, sir," she drawled in a Yorkshire-by-way-of-Flatbush accent. "I'm thinkin' they wouldn't have come to this debacle if they had any good common sense at all!"

"Ouch!" I cringed in my best silent-movie acting, "Forsoothly, thou hast zapped me goodeth!!"

I stopped at Mandy's booth next. It was one of the more creative (which is to say cheaper) ones made up of oak poles and striped canvas that were an enlargement on the one they had used at the Cloisters but made to withstand the run of the show. It had open sides with a massive pole in the center so that it resembled a miniature circus tent.

Persian and pseudo-Persian carpets had been spread inside, and sconces of flowers and throw pillows were scattered about to enhance the Arab bazaar feel of the place.

All around, suspended from cross poles by string, were Mandy's soft sculpture puppets, which made anyone standing in the tent feel like they were being watched by a chorus of little people. Some were just dolls, really, but most were rod puppets with a few genuine marionettes for variety. They were somewhere between grotesque and beautiful and as fascinating as their creator.

"Faith and begorra, sir, if it's not the top of the mornin' to ya!" Robin Madden swaggered up to me. Decked out like Maureen O'Hara in *The Spanish Main*, she exhibited more cleavage than any two women

I'd seen so far that day. She was radiant and seemed born to the period world, and finally seemed truly happy.

"And it's the goose I see you're missing," I returned, feigning being blinded by the expanse of white above her bodice.

"And how's that?"

"Well, God knows you have the sauce already," I said and bowed with my winning pun

She grinned. "I should know better with you than to trade bad puns, Eric," she said with a chuckle.

"The world should know better," I answered, laughing. "You be sure you put sunblock on those glories," I added. For emphasis, I reached over and flicked the silver swan charm on her necklace. "Else we'll have another swan-in-the-valley exhibit."

She blushed a deep red. While most of us end up nut-brown by the end of faire, we work at it gradually to protect our skins. Last season, she hadn't used sunblock at all the first weekend and had been burned badly. The white silhouette of a swan had flown between her breasts half the year.

"No need to worry," Mandy said, emerging from the curtained back room. "She has Conn to keep her well-greased." At the mention of the new boyfriend, Robin blushed deeper, which I didn't think possible. I accepted a joyous hug from Mandy and bent to add a peck to her cheek.

"How's the crowd?"

"Looks good," I said, "as eager to start this damn thing as we are."

"Great," Mandy said, "and to spend vast amounts of money, I hope."

"Amen," I tossed off as I headed out. "I'm off to first scene. See you later."

"Take care," Robin called.

"Ditto!" Mandy added.

I made a quick circuit of the crafters on my way to the first scene of the day's scenario where the highwaymen attack us guards "from ambush" and we have a short sword fight before we are humiliated for the first time in the day and then they escape to plague us for the rest of the day. Evil bad guys just need love too!

My long way around the crafter circuit every day was a pleasant ritual that allowed me to check out the terrain for mud spots, broken glass, and the like in case I had to "call it" for any of the later scenes.

Fighters checked the ground before each scene anyway, but as the captain of the ship, so to speak, I liked to be there first. Also, if conditions were too wet, I had the power (with Dawn and Barry) to call a "wet day," which meant that it was too dangerous to do any of the fighting scenes.

Those days, we had to curtain the big action scenes and move the act indoors under the various awnings since it was rare to ever completely shut the show down.

Fully declared wet days were rare but were very wild. Try to imagine twenty six-year-olds playing indoors and you have an idea of our energy level. The scenes that consisted of just fighting—like the chess game—were cancelled outright. All the other scenes mutated to "draw sword and they surrender" scenarios.

So, of course, on those days, everyone played every scene completely over the top or as one old hand put it, "those were the days that could never be considered kosher for the amount of ham wandering around the faire grounds spouting pseudo-Shakespeare!"

"Hey boss," said Smitty as I got to the "backstage" area behind the barn to "form up" with the other guards. "How's the crowd?"

"Good. I think they might actually want to see us make period fools of ourselves."

"Well," Vita called over from the water barrel, "they came to the right place; we were gonna do it anyway."

The rest of the fight corps finished their warm-ups. This was our "bullpen," where we rehearsed our fights before scenes or just chilled out for five or ten minutes away from the public. Most of the actors used it for cigarette breaks since they couldn't smoke in character on the grounds, so it was also "the smokehouse." Only two of the fight corps smoked, as it turned out, which was usual. Most stage fighters tend to be a physically fit bunch who need their "wind'—though it stops a lot of them from drinking off hours like fish.

"Hey, big guy!" Vita said as she joined me with a quarterstaff in each hand. "Let's do the chess fight, quick. I'm fuzzy on the whirligig move. We won't have that much time later to run the whole thing." Often, we gave pet names to each phase of a fight. It helped with memorization.

"Okay! I said." She tossed me one of the oak staves and we backed off to start. "Let's just mark the flips," I added. "No sense in doing them all out."

High cross. Flynn. The sticks clacked quickly and precisely, though we put no "acting" into the exercise.

"Have you seen Robin's new boyfriend?" I asked.

Poke and get-outta-Dodge. She moved nimbly to avoid a wide swipe. A couple of the fighters wandered over to watch with a critical eye.

"Oh yeah. Not my type, I like 'em big." Her smirk was at the edge of filthy.

Thrust. Pool cue attack.

"And stupid?" I quoted the old song.

Numbers run.

"Hey, hey, that would include you, you know!" she said with no equivocation.

"Oh, I guess it would, but seriously ..."

Whirligig. She got the move perfectly.

"That's it!" I exclaimed. "What's this Conn like?" I praised her but we kept at it to the end.

"Tall, thin, brown hair," Vita said. "Does funny voices. She says he likes all the same books and movies she does; a perfect fit or so it seems."

Reverse Flynn.

"Well, she sure seems happy and that's all that really matters," I said. "I guess I'll finally meet him tonight at the campfire."

Spin demon-flip-finish. Spot-on ending. In the last move it looks like she wins and bang! I flip her. The villain wins the fight! Which starts the general brawl at the chess match.

The watching fighters nodded approval and drifted back to what they had been doing, resting or prepping.

"That seems pretty solid," I said with satisfaction. I extended a hand to help her up.

"You think much about those two guys on the roof?" she whispered when she looked around to be sure we were alone. She was standing beside me, brushing herself off, and avoided eye contact.

"No." I lied. "You okay about it?"

"Oh, yeah," she lied back. "Just, well, I've never seen anyone shot except in movies and stuff."

"Neither have I," I said. "You having nightmares?" I'd had some but hadn't told anyone, even Krystal, about them.

"Actually no," she said sincerely, "I just—you know, it's creepy." She looked up at me with very blue eyes. "I think we did the right thing not reporting it. Would've just got us messed up in legal stuff for nothing but still...."

"Yeah, I know," I answered. We stood for a long moment, saying nothing, letting the sounds of the faire swirl around us. It seemed as if she might say something more but I spoke first.

"Hey, we have a show to do!" I shrugged it off and grabbed Dave Burton, my fight partner for the first scene. She was tight-lipped but just nodded her head; she knew me well enough to know it all bothered me, but I had no answers either.

The first scene was another piece of theatre Shakespeare would have both been ashamed of and completely understood as needed to "please the groundlings" with the low comedy elements in it.

It was where I got tripped in the usual "me dumb guard" fashion, and the day was back on track. I was able to keep my mind mostly off the world outside the faire during the day and I liked it that way.

———

All the actors carried a little 4"x5" typed card called a route sheet. It listed each scene we had, the location (King's Stage, chess board, tavern, etc.) and the time in fifteen-minute increments from eleven o'clock 'til closing at six. Even breaks had to be scheduled so that the village was always teeming with actors in character to keep the audience in the illusion.

The general scenario for the day was the evil King's Guards try to oppress the peasants (at the behest of the evil duke) and the good highwaymen led by Dick Turpin (as I've mentioned this Ren faire stuff was ahistorical) defeat them at every turn.

There were various supporting characters, both good and archly sinister, and in the end, right (not to mention capitalist producers) was triumphant. Three action scenes that more or less advanced the plot followed the first scene set around the faire so that everyone got a chance to get the broad facts of the storyline, then we guards had a short break.

The biggest scene I was in contained a twenty-eight-move rapier fight I did with Dick Turpin himself. Of course I lost in a humiliating way as usual. Then, I had half an hour to prepare for the human chess match.

The living chess match was a fixture at many Ren faires and the highlight of many. It was a pure fight show with the thin framework of a chess game between the duke and the king performed on a huge "board" defined with sand and white chalk. It was performed before crowds that hit five thousand on capacity days.

The good guys' side was composed of Dick Turpin's boys, some townspeople, and a few hearty peasants. The bad guys were my guards, the Duke's faithful executioner, and some of the "dark" townspeople characters.

We fought with every variation of weapon we could think of and in every style from commedia clowning to down and dirty fistfights that bordered on tragedy. It was a great showcase for my choreography and the skill of the fighters I'd hired.

The last fight was between my character (in the "evil duke" livery) and Kelly for Dick Turpin's boys. My character cheated, of course, and so was challenged to a joust of honor at the end of the day.

At two thirty, after the chess game was over, I hid in the back of Mandy's tent and ate like a horse.

"Whoa, big fella," she said. "Take a breath. Here's some iced tea."

"Thanks, hon." I smiled at her from the comfy throw pillow where I was seated Indian-style. She bustled into the little sheik's den back room and sat down beside me. "Careful," I warned, "don't get your fingers too close to my mouth."

She brightened into an evil smile and ventured to run her right pointer finger along my lips. Of course, I called her bluff and gobbled her finger to the second knuckle. Her wicked smile traveled to her eyes.

"Well," she whispered, "now that you've got me, what are you going to do with me?"

I growled, released her finger and said gruffly, "Nothing 'til I find some ketchup!" We both laughed.

"You're killing me," I said in a tone that bordered on serious.

She deflected that right away with "The little death?"

"I wasn't going there," I said. When she looked at me from under hooded eyes I laughed. "Okay, well, not intentionally anyway."

"I thought things with you and Krystal are going strong?"

"Oh, they are," I replied, "but I am only human and you are a domestic goddess, after all."

She gave a little bow. "Thank you for noticing."

"Speaking of connubial bliss," I said, "I hear Robin's got a winner this time."

Mandy grew suddenly serious. "I think she might have. He's clever, funny, and really seems to dote on her. God knows she needs that."

"Wow," I stammered, "high praise indeed coming from you."

She nodded. "I know. Myself, I'm waiting to find out if he's an embezzler or something." She laughed. "She hasn't been this happy in a long time."

"That's good," I said quietly. "We all need to see some happiness around here." We were quiet for a minute. She leaned against me and we hugged.

"Okay," I added, "I meant some new happiness."

"That's better." She smiled.

"Oh, I'm sorry," a male said from the tent doorway. "Robin said to store my gear back here." His voice was soft, maybe soft enough to have a trace of Belfast underneath. He was backlit and it was difficult to see details, but he appeared to be thin, raw-boned, and I guessed about six foot. As he moved away from the tent opening, I noticed his neat red beard. He wore scruffy jeans, with a million keys and a small flashlight on his belt.

"Speak of the charming devil," Mandy said. "Eric, this is Conn O'Malley." I rose to step out into the sunlight to shake his hand. He had a firm grip, long delicate fingers and a grin that had enough of the old country rogue in it to remind me of Tom.

"Hi," I said, "I almost met you on a dead run at Mandy's about two weeks ago—I was running late to the soap opera."

"God-of-me fathers, I recall," he joked. "I was laden with woman, child and groceries as the tall blur went racing down the stairs." He had a relaxed, easy manner.

"Let me just dump this," he added as he moved across the tent with a slight limp in his left leg and dropped a backpack in the corner. "You're the fella that's playing Lancelot later, eh?"

"Guilty," I quipped, gobbling up the last of my curly fries. "But I'm more Mordredish."

"How the hell do you do that and stay alive?" he asked with a little laugh.

"Very carefully," I answered. "We use steel shields for the pine lance hits and half balsa lances for the hits on the chest."

"On the chest? Ouch!" Conn winced theatrically.

"With Kevlar vest over a karate chest protector."

"Clever."

"Well, there are bold jousters and there are old jousters. There are no old, bold jousters." At that, we all laughed.

"I'd better be getting along," I said. "Next scene!"

"See you later." Mandy smiled.

"Good to finally meet you," Conn said, extending his hand again. "Nice to see you live up to the legend the ladies spin about you."

I shook his hand and grinned. "It's nice to hear that the money I pay them to advertise me as a near deity is paying off. Come on backstage anytime," I offered. "I'll show you how we play King Arthur and live to tell the tale."

"Maybe later in the summer," he said. "I'm looking forward to seeing the show from out front with my lady fair."

I nodded, pecked Mandy on the cheek and hurried out.

Once outside, I noted that Robin was writing up a credit card purchase. I leaned over her shoulder and whispered in her ear. "Bingo on this one, kiddo." She blushed with appreciation.

There was still the Shakespeare play and some minor scenes for the crowd to enjoy, but the last two hours of the day were less "scene dense" to allow the attendees to make some purchases and then jockey for good seats at the tilt field and wait for the joust. After the chess game, I had no responsibilities but preparing for the joust, which was good because there was usually a lot to do. This was especially true in the first couple of weeks as we were all getting used to the new routine.

Jousting, historically, was sort of the off-season training for the warrior knights of Europe, a way to stay in fighting shape between wars. In fact, there were periods of time when the fatalities from "sport" jousts outdistanced the nobility's battlefield casualties in a number of countries, with France losing a king to injuries sustained on the "sport" jousting field.

"Hey, cowboy," Red O'Boyle called to me when I entered the stable to check on Whiskey's tack gear. She had a big smile on her face and an evil twinkle in her eye. "Dawn wants to do the victory lap after all."

"Oh, sugar honey iced tea!" I blurted out.

Our lovely, coked-up producer had a personal fantasy that she had the power to impose on all of us. It involved riding on the saddle of the winning knight and waving princess-like to the adoring crowds (and showing off her non-period Gucci shoes for all to see).

Unfortunately, that meant Kelly had to ride her, since he played the good guy. It was unfortunate because the not-so-rhinestone cowboy absolutely could not stand the little princess.

"Have you told Kelly?" I asked, knowing already she had not or else I would have heard the screaming already.

"No," Red said, shrugging and smiling more at me. "I'm a coward."

"I'll do it," I said grudgingly. "I owe you."

"This'll make us even."

"I'll say it will." I kept walking through the barn, past the rack where we kept the pine lances and the cabinet where the balsa breakaways were stored. We only fitted a four-foot balsa piece to a lock socket on the end of a pine lance for the body hit. A longer balsa piece was unstable and might shatter before the hit. "DLS: droopy lance syndrome," Vita had nicknamed it.

Kelly was already suited up for the ride. He wore a long tabard over a fake chainmail shirt made of rope sprayed silver and elbow pads hidden under the sleeves. He wore no chest protector since I was on the receiving end of the lance. Why should we both sweat our balls off?

I proceeded to strip off my doublet and shirt and had a cool drink of Gatorade. "How's the horses?" I asked, searching for a way to ease into the news about Dawn.

"Fine," he said. "Both rarin' to go; I checked all the new tack and it's all looking good." He adjusted his metal collar, the gorget, which was both throat protector and neck brace. We both wore them and had padded the inside with foam for comfort, but it was still a necessary pain.

"Nice for things to work out smooth for a change," I said. I was trying hard to think how to break the Dawn rider scenario to him.

"Just one little thing, though," Kelly added. He kind of squinted at me with his head at an angle. I knew from experience that it wasn't a positive look.

What now, I thought.

"What's up?"

"Carlos had to go home, suddenly. His mother's sick. Nothin' life-threatening, but he had to go—I told him he could. He'll be gone for most of, if not the whole summer." Kelly was all "aw shucks" at the same time he continued to arm up, all business. It was the most I've ever heard him say at a single time.

Carlos was Kelly's second, like Smitty was mine. The seconds are our cornermen checking our equipment, picking up fallen weapons, and making the ride if we can't for some reason. After all, the show must go on!

"How are we gonna manage the horse? I guess we can pull Vita from her melee fight, but—" My head was spinning with all that would have to be changed around without someone dedicated to the horses and our weapons. "And what the hell are we gonna do for backup?" I asked.

I tried not to let my concern make my question sharp, but I was in charge and the good of the show rested, ultimately, on my shoulders. This was a big monkey wrench.

"I got a guy who's been hangin' around," Kelly said with a little shrug. "You mighta seen him; his name is Max. He's a guy I met at the stables over in Greenwood Lake and he's been helping me and Smitty with the horses. He's a good rider."

"He hasn't even had a full run-through with us, and we're going out in front of paying customers," I blurted out. If Kelly said the guy was a good rider, he was, but the fact is that the joust was a finely tuned and deliberately choreographed affair. Throwing a new element in with no rehearsal was risky. "Can he fight?"

"Don't know," my cowboy cohort shrugged, "but Smitty can learn both sides and be first to cover either of us. It's harder to find someone who can handle the horses than fight. Besides, the chances of both of us being out on the same day are better than me finding a third wife who'll put up with me."

I slipped my fake chainmail shirt over my chest protector and belted it on while I thought it over. I knew Kelly had thought this out and could tell he wasn't happy with telling me, but I also knew he would not have let Carlos go if it wasn't the right thing to do.

"Good enough for now," I said with a shrug and a resigned smile. "We'll deal with it later; let's finish here and go huddle up to talk Max through this first one."

He helped me buckle on my gorget. The metal collar acted as an anchor point for our helmets to fit into, in addition to protection for our throats.

I grabbed my sixteen-gauge steel helmet and put my arm around Kelly's shoulder as we walked to the horses.

"Well then," I said with a jolly smile and an evil chuckle, "I have something special to tell you as well."

116

There is no adequate way to describe what it's like to ride in a joust. The most accurate word would be glorious, but it still doesn't quite convey the feelings I experienced each time I suited up, climbed on a horse's back, and rode out to perform.

Capacity crowd was seven thousand "civilians," though once, when the Jersey beaches were closed for a sewage spill, the greedy producers managed to squeeze ten thousand bodies around the tilting field.

The pattern of the joust settled into a comfortable pattern early on and followed the template most jousts did; equally based on the rules of the joust from old manuscripts and Hollywood B-movies.

It started with Bob, the drummer, on a timpani base drum beating out a martial rhythm. Then two horns took up the call. Ta-da-da-da!

At that point, the crowd begins to stir. Fathers, just as excited as sons, tingle as if before a playoff game; girlfriends giggle and squeeze their boyfriends' arms and snuggle closer in anticipation of seeing a real knight in shining armor.

The King's Box and Reviewing Stand is located dead center of the field on one side and is garishly colorful, with banners and pennants hanging from it. All the main players of the day were present and in their court finery with bright blues, gold and crimson being the main colors. King Stephen's opera-trained voice boomed out after the horn fanfare with, "Bring forth the noble knights!"

The new guy, Max, who had replaced Carlos, slipped into his role easily in the last joust of that first day. The tall blond opened the gate at one end, and Smitty opened the gate at the other end.

Kelly and I rocketed out onto the field with the two horses under us remembering the thrill and anxious to play with each other.

The crowd went wild! Screaming, cheering, and yelling our character names. We circled the field twice, waving (or in my case) snarling at the crowd.

The sound, the scent, the wave of that thunderous crowd against my gut is a feeling that makes the blood roar in your ears—races your pulse—makes you feel like Charlemagne, Lancelot, and Richard Coeur de Leon all rolled into one. It's completely intoxicating, and I make no apologies for it. Somebody gave me a joke t-shirt once that said, "Born to tilt." No joke. I have lived this before!

We reined up the horses before the king and lowered our lances to receive the blessing from the bishop (Norman, a Jewish musical theater actor).

Then the ladies tied colorful "favors" to our arms; light silk scarves that would flow behind us like contrails on a jet.

We two knights rode off our ends of the field with our horses facing away from each other.

Our squires, Smitty and the graceful Max, raced out, secured our helms and shields, did a final check of our tack gear and then took up positions in our respective corners holding the horse's heads.

My world at that point was reduced to the view out the narrow slit of the helmet. My breath rasping heavily inside the armor was like the sound of a bellows. The crowd's roar sounded as a distant thunderous rumble over a mountain range, almost drowned out by the creak of the leather tack gear and the pounding of my own heart.

The king signaled with a wave of his hand that got the trumpeters and Bob going.

Smitty gave me the nod and released Whiskey's head (purposely positioned away from Crusader because both horses, sighting each other, just go for it). The tack harness creaked louder as I wheeled Whiskey left. He sighted his playmate, snorted, and spurs were completely unnecessary.

A couple of thousand pounds of horses and men thundered across the field toward each other as the crowd screams even louder. By then, I was deaf and blind to anything but the two-foot target of Kelly's shield and the rhythm of my own breath.

Bang! My lance point hit high and outside to glance off his shield. He dropped his posture and played at a stagger in the saddle.

We circled the whole field to our original corners while the crowd cheers became even louder. There were days that I wondered that any of them had a voice when they left the faire grounds.

My breathing always grew staccato by that point. I always worry about having an asthma attack, but somehow I always get through. That day was no different.

We made a second pass and repeated it all, with Kelly dropping his lance and changing his posture to play wounded.

I switched lances as he rearmed with the breakaway handed him by the new guy. The two squires stood holding the horses' heads again, hands raised 'til we both say we're ready for the last pass. The horses were harder to control at that point, excited to be playing the running-at-each-other game and anxious to do it again.

Then, with an arm drop signal, we were off!

Fifty feet: I opened my shield position to expose my left chest.

Thirty feet: Kelly targeted low and to the outside.

Ten feet: Kelly stood in the stirrups to brace for impact. I shifted my feet to toes only, ready to let go.

Impact! It was like taking a football tackle, with some lineman's head spearing me dully under the left pec.

I lost the shield and lance and leaned right to fall away from Crusader's path. We used to lose the old pot helmets as well at that point, but I never liked the look and our new pig-snout visors took the fall fine with a little better protection for our heads.

I did a dive shoulder roll off the horse. I hit the ground a little hard but manageably, then purposely lost my helmet in the roll so the audience could see my evil face in defeat. I made one vain attempt to rise then fell back and lay as if stunned.

Whiskey was caught by Max, and Kelly rode back leisurely to point his shattered lance at me and proclaim, "You are fairly defeated, sirrah, do you yield?"

At that point, I reared up and pulled him from his horse, and we fought. I got a sword; he had just his shield. We made it all big and showy moves with lots of growling while the crowd cheered and chanted our character names.

Thirty moves later, I lost and was knocked cold. I welcomed the rest, laying on the dusty ground, breathing hard.

The crowd screamed their heads off as I was helped off the field by fellow guardsmen.

Then, Dawn, flashing her anachronistic pumps, was helped to the saddlebow by two hefty highwaymen. Kelly smiled through clenched teeth and they were off to do the victory lap.

By the numbers, letter perfect.
God save the King!
Tom would have loved it.

Chapter Eleven

B y the time the faire was up and running, I was long back to working at the health club all mid-week and doing occasional soap opera work for real cash. (Though I love it, Ren faire life is not lucrative.)

In the weeks that followed, all of our lives settled into a pleasant regularity. Jillian gained strength during that summer, losing the always-haunted look in her eyes and even putting on some healthy weight. Robin and Conn continued to be a solid item and were a fixture around the campfires of the faire. Krystal came up for a visit once in August for a long weekend to see the show (and test the integrity of my tent). Max turned out to be a good worker as a squire, learned the riding routine competently and I felt better about him, even if he proved a little sullen and aloof.

I didn't forget what I'd promised Jill and myself about finding out what had really happened to Tom, or that two men had died on the roof of his building trying to kill me. In fact I thought about it constantly.

The Wednesday before the last weekend of the faire in September found me and Vita at A.C.'s school.

"When you've finished," I signaled A.C, who was leading a class, "come in the office."

Vita and I pulled chairs up to his desk in the small room to wait. Dressed for her day job as a secretary, Vita wore a gauze skirt, white cotton blouse and high-heeled sandals. Her skin glowed a chestnut brown and her blonde hair was bleached almost platinum from weekends spent in the sun.

I had come straight from the set of a soap opera without changing. I had been cast as a Mafia hitman who had some lines. This meant I had my hair slicked back, wore a fake but real-looking facial scar and was dressed all in black with a red silk tie. A.C. walked into his office five minutes later and shook his head.

"You white folks are driving property values down!"

"Just shut the door, A.C.," I said in a tired voice. "Vita has the lists." He closed the door with a serious expression falling across his face.

Vita spread white cards on the desk. I'd asked Vita to check the buildings whose doors backed onto the alley in Chinatown where I'd lost Mr. Gunns two months ago. It wasn't like we had a plethora of clues so I had gone back to where it all started.

"From the downstairs signboards?" A.C. asked

"From all three buildings," Vita said, "and either I or Rick checked each door as we walked past."

I had pursued the only other area of investigation I could think of by checking in with every bookie in Brooklyn and all those I could turn up near Tom's printing plant, and they all agreed with Tondinelli: Tom seemed to have really gone on the straight and narrow. Every one of them had a good opinion of him and he had made good on any debts months before his death. He only bought the weekly lottery ticket that Jill knew about. Poppo got his sources to back up my findings. That left me scratching my metaphorical head and at a loss for any motive or suspects.

For a long time afterward, I sat in a McDonald's on Canal Street sipping a Coke and staring at the storefronts across the street, feeling like the worst would-be gumshoe that had ever been. I watched people going in and out of buildings, making up stories to myself about who they were and why they were on the street, until I saw a woman realtor meeting with some businessman. She wore her little company jacket, and I could see even across the street that she was giving the guy a heck of a pitch for the building they were standing in front of. After a time, she led him to the old metal door.

"Hope you make the sale, honey," I thought. "Good luck selling anything in this economy—"

Then I was struck by a sudden inspiration.

Sales! Every building had an owner, and owners had names and addresses!

I went to the office of the city engineer and talked to a bunch of civil service drones to get access to city records to research the ownership of the three buildings that backed onto the alley. The corporations named in the paperwork, unfortunately, were just names: The Red Dragon Realty, The Lucky Charms Corporation, and Yan Bin Realty.

"This is a week's worth of lunch hour work," Vita took pains to remind us as we organized the cards on the desk. "Any of the doors that opened I wandered in looking for a bathroom," she said.

"Yup, that's you, Vita Kitalis, fastest bladder in the east!"

I ducked fast and just avoided a Lithuanian knuckle sandwich.

"I don't see any pattern or clue, as such," A.C. said, "but that doesn't mean something is not here. So—*Im Jun Moe Tae*: let's keep at it." We looked through Vita's notes and recollections of what was in each office she had visited. She had a pretty good memory and had made detailed notes about what she and Rick had seen but I was afraid my last straw to grasp at was blowing away in the wind of logic.

"This is hopeless," I said, two cans of coke and three slices of pizza later. "What the hell does an international killer have to do with knock-off Power Ranger dolls or chopstick import companies?"

"Don't forget the place that makes the inflatable bras," Vita said. This time, she ducked just ahead of my swing.

"We're all too toasted to think logically," A.C. said. "Let's try this again tomorrow."

He didn't have to say it twice.

An idea almost flashed through my mind, one of those glimmers of thought that were just beyond the sight of the mind's eye yet so fleeting that they begged to be called back. But I really was too tired to chase it. I was also still restless so I said, "I wanna work the bag a bit. I'm still all keyed up from the set."

"Sure," A.C. said. "Just remember to lock up. I'm gonna shower and crash. "Nite, Vee." I walked Vita downstairs.

"I really appreciate you making those trips to get the info, Vee," I said. She grinned like an urchin.

"Hey, I'm Honey West reincarnated," she said. "It's my destiny, and besides, what's family for?"

I gave her a long hug. Her loyalty made me feel good but my inability to find any other leads to the men who killed Tom was making me feel pretty inadequate.

Back upstairs, I took off my shirt and shoes, put on some gloves and took my frustrations out on the heavy bag. And frustrations I had plenty.

I was, as the pundits say, clueless. Stopped dead in the water, with no way to find either Mr. Gunns or Blondie. All I had were those three buildings and the insane certainty that they would lead me to the men who killed Tom, but no idea how.

I worked the bag hard, slamming my fists into it till the shock of my knuckles jarred my teeth. I pounded it until I was pouring sweat and winded, but divine inspiration was not forthcoming.

I kept rolling all the information I had over and over in my head till it all blurred before my eyes. Tommy Gunns and his fashion plate thug danced in my head like hideous sugarplums and I envisioned them under my fists and tried to beat an answer out of them.

On a hunch I'd asked Poppo to forward the ballistics report on the two guys from Tom's roof to the Brits. Just a stab in the dark, but it paid off. That gun had also been used in three killings in Belfast: two suspected IRA sympathizers and a twelve-year-old Protestant girl. It was a piece of information besides the list of offices that didn't seem to fit into the situation at all.

All it did was confirm that I was up against some real bad boys.

"This is useless," I said aloud after a particularly lousy punch that hurt my wrist. "I'd have to have the deductive skills of Sherlock Holmes or Merlin's magic to make sense of this mess."

I froze suddenly as a blast of divine inspiration, like Zeus's fire, hit me right between the eyes. I shook my head to clear it and found myself staring at my fists like a complete idiot.

"It can't be that simple," I said aloud. The more I thought about it, though, the more the answer seemed to jump out at me.

"Wake up!" I banged on A.C.'s door minutes later. "I've got it!"

Imagine stumbling into a sleeping bear's den and then screaming "hunting season" in its ear. That will give you some idea of what A.C. looked like when he opened the door to his office.

"What?" he demanded in a voice that was almost a growl.

"What breakfast cereal is magically delicious?" I asked. It's a tribute to our long friendship that he didn't try to kill me on the spot.

"What?"

"No, no I'm serious." I whistled the commercial jingle to the cereal and did the little dance step that went with it. "Magically delicious," I finished.

"Uh … Lucky Charms?" I watched A.C.'s gaze measure me for a straitjacket as I pushed past him and hurried to his desk. Vita's note cards were still spread out.

"Here … look!" I pointed frantically to one of the cards. "The Lucky Charms Corporation."

Now A.C. was awake.

"Only a sick mind that would use a name like Tommy Gunns for an arms dealer—" I said.

A.C. finished the thought. "And that's same kind of sick mind that would name his company for a cartoon leprechaun."

"They are listed as the owners of the building and have an office in the building on the third floor," I added. "Vita said it was a steel door locked with an outside padlock."

A.C. stared at me again, but differently now.

"What?" I studied him. "You think I'm crazy? I know it's a coincidence, but it's just too good."

"I think you're dead-on," A.C. said quietly. "I think anybody else, any fully *sane* person, would have missed it." He sat on an office chair and worked to rub sleep out of his eyes.

"I want to go there. Now." I expected an argument but surprisingly didn't get one.

"Okay," he said. "Let me just get a few things together we might need."

For a moment I was too stunned to react to the fact that I didn't have to argue with him, then my mind started racing.

While A.C. "got his things together," I called Jillian at Mandy's place. Robin answered. She and her beau, Conn, were keeping Jill company while Mandy and Don were out at some event at the Society of Illustrators. (We all still were worried enough about her to see that she wasn't left alone for long)

When Jill came on the phone, I told her as matter-of-factly as I could what I had surmised and what I was going to do.

She was quiet for a moment and tried not to sound too motherly when she did speak, but said, "You promise you're just going to take a look around and be careful?"

"I promise, mama De Dannin, I'll just poke my nose in and then get my butt home."

"Okay then," she said, "go gettum!"

I didn't have the heart to tell her I'd talked A.C. into going too.

A.C. and I took the train to Chinatown, sitting silently, still stunned by the thought that we were going to the "nest" of the vipers that had killed Tom. Or at least, that's how I thought about it.

It was still teeming with activity, even at midnight on a Wednesday.

A.C.'s gathered "things" turned out to be a little bag of burglar's tools—souvenirs from his "hoodlum youth" days. He always gave a little chuckle when he said that and was never sure how serious he was about it—at least not until that night.

Although I'd splashed water on myself, my hair was still slicked down and the latex scar was still in place. I was still in my dark suit and A.C. had on black kick jeans and a leather jacket. As we hurried along without saying a word, I'm sure we looked for all the world like Shaft and Scarface out for a stroll.

A.C. had been silent on the train as well. I couldn't blame him. We were going to commit a crime. Regardless of motive, it was still a crime. Me, Captain Straight, on my way to break into the office of The Lucky Charms Corporation. Even for Tom's sake, it was hard to banish the voice of the Lone Ranger who admonished, *"Don't break the law."*

"We're going in without any recon," A.C. said when we stood in the alley facing the trio of doors. "You know we really are doing this the stupid way, don't you?"

"Yeah, I know." I looked at him and shrugged. "We can still turn around and go home if you think it's too stupid."

"Hell, no," he said and gave me a rare, warm smile. "You don't have inspirations often enough that I can afford to ignore them."

We went to the fire door of the building and my education in burglary began. "These fire doors are usually not really airtight in these old buildings," A.C. said. "It's the best choice for covert entry."

To be fair about his "criminal past," A.C. had also taught the Seals how to fight house to house, so some of his abilities of the night he could have come by honestly.

A.C. slipped a device made of an old coat hanger into a crack he found at one edge of the door and, after a few tries, hooked the panic bar and yanked the door open.

He grinned like a magician who had just pulled a rabbit out of his hat.

"We're lucky they didn't chain the inside closed."

"And that there was no alarm!"

"Vita said there was none on any of these doors." He smiled again. "She does good work."

"I've told her so often." I nodded. "But I'll add your praise to the bouquet I buy her for this one."

We entered soundlessly and went up the stairs directly to the third floor, where The Lucky Charms Corporation had its office. The corridor was an unhealthy brown color, repulsive even in the dimness of the night lighting. The wide hallway had carpeting that looked as old as the building, which would make it about a hundred and change. It didn't smell all that fresh, either.

The sliding, loading dock-type office door was as Vita described it—steel with a wide metal strip across it and locked with a large padlock. It was painted a bright green with "Lucky Charms Corp" stenciled on it.

"Real subtle," A.C. whispered. He looked over at me and nodded, "I do think you have it right, Eric; from here on out, we are going into some dark waters. You still up for what comes?"

I swallowed hard. "Yeah, *Im Jun Moe Tae!*"

"Hwa Rang!" he added and grinned.

He knelt by the lock and went to work using a pick and tension wrench. He'd also done security for that escape artist guy, Locke. "There could be an alarm in here," he said.

But we were lucky, there were no wires or alarm switches of any kind.

"Anything in particular you're looking for?" A.C. asked as he slid the door back.

"A horse head?" I shrugged. "How do I know, this is my first illegal entry."

He laughed evilly. "Cherry!"

The office consisted of a large outer room with two sturdy workbenches and a vise on one of them. The inner room contained a desk, two chairs, and an old-style man-sized safe.

"No," A.C. said when we saw the safe. "Don't even think it, I'm not Jimmy Valentine."

"The desk, then."

I started in the outer office and looked through the debris scattered on the workbenches: screws and washers of various sizes, and slivers of metal littered the top.

"Notice something odd?" A.C. asked as he walked into the other room.

I shook my head. "There are no personal items anywhere in the room—no girlie calendars, kids' pictures, or mementos. Nadda!"

"Not a happy office," I muttered.

A.C. emerged from the inner office. "Nothing in there. It's picked clean as well. Almost feels like nobody really works here."

"Well, they do." I picked up a small piece of metal I spotted on the floor near the foot of the workbench. "And now I know what they do."

A.C. took the two-inch piece of rectangular stamped metal from me and studied it. "Is this what I think it is?"

128

"Yes," I said through clenched teeth. "It's part of a conversion kit for a MAC-10 from semi-auto to full auto."

"You sure?" he asked as he held it up to the light and tried to imagine it fitting into the automatic weapon.

"When I did that war picture two years ago, I hung out with the weapons guy. He showed me how to do the conversion, and I did some for him. That is definitely what that little baby is."

"No question what's in that safe then; gotta be their converted stock. That stuff is very, very illegal," A.C. said.

"Yeah, but let's not push our luck." I wiped fingerprints off the piece of metal before we left.

A.C. locked the padlock when we were in the hall again. "I'm gonna bust my bladder if I don't whiz," he said and made a beeline for the men's room two doors down the hall.

"What the hell do I do while you drain your lizard?" I asked.

"Do that leprechaun dance if you want," he snickered. "I'm busy; I'll be right out."

There I stood—alone in the hall of the building in front of the office we'd just burgled. Talk about awkward!

To pass the time, I decided to try my hand at picking the lock—just to see if I could. I still had A.C.'s lock pick tools so I took a shot at it. What did I have to lose?

I slipped two of the picks out of the little case and knelt down to peer at the lock closely. I wasn't really sure where to begin—it isn't like you see on TV—you have to use the pick and a little doohickey called a tension wench to hold the tumblers aside once you "work them," that much I knew from watching A.C. but still I wasn't really sure what to do.

As it turns out, it didn't really matter because while I was absorbed in staring at the lock, things changed.

"Hallo! What have we here?" It was a slight Cork-by-way-of-London accent.

I looked up to see three guys standing at the opposite end of the hallway.

Oh crap! I thought. *I'm in a whole lot of trouble!* I couldn't tell them I was looking for a contact lens with a lock pick kit in my hand.

They approached with an unhurried walk, an air of menace about them that sent a chill up my spine. The one in the middle pointed an automatic pistol at my head and smiled. It was Mr. Gunns.

Face on, close up, Mister Gunns was not the monster my mind had manufactured—he was just an average-looking man, wearing a light windbreaker and a baseball cap pulled down over neatly cut brown hair. His manner was as calm as if he were looking over a menu.

"Now, who the hell are you, mate?" he asked.

Interesting ... Mr. Gunns didn't recognize me, and I didn't see the need to help him any. I pitched my voice a little nasal and did my best realistic version of a Rocky voice. "Tony Baretta," I answered. "Who the hell are you?"

"Search him," he ordered. The two hooligans—each with the map of Ireland clearly stamped on their faces—moved to either side of me. They were very professional in staying out of Gunns's line of fire while they stepped in to frisk me.

They patted me down as roughly as they could but found only ten bucks in cash and an expired metro card. A.C. and I had left all of our IDs back in the alley in a prophetic moment of "just in case."

"What are you doing here?" he asked. He had a feminine mouth and no meanness in his manner, no false tough guy bravado at all. He was calm and relaxed as if we were just shooting the breeze. His amber eyes, however, revealed the true man behind them. Those eyes were the coldest eyes I'd ever seen. Killer eyes.

"Brian, help the nice lad find a voice," he said in a jovial tone.

"Right, Johnnie," the one to my left said. His accent said he was American. He had a broken tooth in the front that he displayed with a wide grin at being given the task. He also had a mean left hook that slammed into my gut at about a hundred miles an hour.

I couldn't breathe for what felt like a long time and coughed until I dry-heaved.

"Ready to give a civil answer, mate?" Johnnie asked the son-of-a-bitch-formerly-known as Tommy Gunns. He was crouched low to look me in the eyes. "Like why are you trying to break into me office; what are you after?"

He thinks I haven't gotten in yet, I thought, *and they have no idea about A.C. being in the can.*

Aloud I said, "Money. I figured any place locked up tight'd have money on hand. You jamokes gonna turn me over to da cops?" (All the time I was thinking, *I can't believe Robert Blake really spoke like this in* Baretta *and people believed him.*)

"Turn you over to the coppers? Ha, funny that," Johnnie said, with a laugh that was chilling in its casualness. He backhanded me with his gun. "We have funny habit we do, of taking care of things ourselves." He stepped back and said, "Okay, boys." Then the real beating started.

It was a simple old-fashioned beating, really, involving a lot of body shots and one particularly nasty punch to the nuts that almost got me puking. I almost passed out on that, but they knew what they were doing and kept me just at the edge. For some reason they stayed mostly away from my face, maybe so they could eventually question me.

"This is fun," the guy on my right said.

"Shut up, Petie," Brian ordered.

After about a hundred years of pain, there was a lull so that the red spots abated, and I was able to see again. Brian and Petie lifted me to my knees to stare up into a crouching Johnnie's cold eyes.

"Now then, mate," Johnnie said mildly. "You're gonna tell us who sent you or we'll take you into the workshop and use a drill on your knees like those IRA bastards used to back in bloody Belfast."

He stared straight into my eyes. His gaze was unblinking, leaving no room for doubt that he was serious.

I thought about Tom and wondered if he had been looking into these same cold pits of amber when his life had been stolen.

That got me angry. A little flame of hate for Johnnie grew in the pit of my stomach and spread through my body like acid.

I don't say what I did next was either heroic or cunningly planned. In fact, fear was as much behind it as anger but that I lived to write this is probably proof of a higher power that took mercy on me.

I suddenly let my body collapse inward and to the right so that Brian, taken off-guard, pitched forward into Johnnie.

Almost at the same instant, I lurched forward, violently pulling Petie with me.

I had no idea what to do next because, as I said, I had no plan, but A.C. solved that for me. He cut the lights.

When things went black, I reacted by instinct. I threw myself backward, taking Petie with me but pulling free of Brian. I heard the bathroom door fly open and A.C.'s footsteps coming my way.

"Let go of me, you goon!" I yelled as a clue for A.C. He got my message and grabbed Petie off me. I heard a sound like a two-by-four hitting a melon, and then I felt A.C.'s iron grip on my upper arms.

"Geez, let go, Petie," I called out, at the same time squeezing A.C.'s hand to let him know I wasn't talking to him.

I did my best stab at mimicking Petie's pained voice and yelled, "Don't shoot, Johnnie, I … uh … got 'em."

A.C. patted me on the shoulder, and we moved down the hall toward our "hosts." I had my left hand on the wall, my right on A.C.'s shoulder. I knew he had his right on the wall.

"Where are you, Petie?" Johnnie yelled, a little annoyance under his calm tone, "Fix the bloody lights, Brian! Get Knight! Now!"

Johnnie Gunns was right in front of me. It was too good an opportunity to miss. I reached forward to where I guessed his hands (and gun) would be. I touched metal first with my left hand, reached over with my right to grab the gun's slide and twisted the gun out of his hand. At the same time, I launched the hardest low swing kick of my life with my right. My foot connected with the inside of his right knee with much more than the four and a half pounds of pressure necessary to snap his kneecap right off. Johnnie screamed like you'd expect. He also went down.

I had the gun now and I grabbed his hair in my left hand and gave him a vicious backhand with the right. The one I had the gun in.

It was a very satisfying feeling.

Beside me, A.C. was fighting Brian. I could hear them grappling on the floor. Johnnie was whimpering and cursing at the same time. I fumbled in his jacket pocket and found a wallet. I grabbed it.

Johnnie latched onto my left shirtsleeve with desperate strength. I clubbed his hand three or four times with the automatic until I heard bones crunch and he let go.

I jumped over him, stumbled, regained my balance, and leaned against the wall in an effort to keep my insides where they belonged. The grunting and smacking behind me had given way to quiet moans.

"Yo, Adrienne," I chanced.

"Here," A.C. said. He found me and slipped an arm around my shoulders. He half-dragged, half-carried me down the stairs to the alley. We retrieved our wallets from the place we'd hidden them. I cleaned my prints off the gun and tossed it back into the building. We walked for ten blocks with A.C. all but carrying me.

"You were born under a lucky star," A.C. said while we sat in a McDonald's on Canal Street. "I found the fuse box in the john but didn't dare move 'til you went postal. Nice hip throw, by the way."

"Lucky star?" I whispered. "They beat the shit out of me." I was shaking violently and beginning to feel the pain as the shock wore off.

"You want to go to St. Vincent's ER?" he asked.

"No," I said. "I don't want anything on record."

"Let's get you home, then," A.C. said. "I'll call Master Yum to stop over."

I was in no shape to argue, but I did get him to stop at a street phone. "I got the bastard's wallet," I told A.C. It was actually more a small portfolio.

We looked through it and found two passports in two different names, credit cards in three names, and three hundred bucks in cash that would buy a lot of aspirin, which I would need. But the bonus was a piece of paper with an address in the Irish section of the Bronx handwritten on it.

"What do we do with these?" A.C. asked.

"Put a big hurt on the son of a bitch." I hissed.

I got the number from information for the New York FBI office and called it. It was a recording menu that shuffled me to a live operator. I gave as my name one of Johnnie's aliases and then (in his voice) confessed to smuggling guns, killing the three people in Belfast, and told them where the Chinatown office was. "You'd better hurry, mate," I said. "I can't live with me guilt but my partners may try to empty the place tonight." Although the operator tried to question me, I hung up. I knew the recording they must have made wouldn't hold up in court but it would get them thinking.

Then, I called the ATF and did the same thing as a concerned citizen. Finally, I called 911 and told the operator I had seen a burglary in progress and that I'd seen guns.

Afterward, we raced (well, I staggered and A.C. dragged me) to the train that we took up to Fifty-Ninth Street. By then I was shivering with shock and couldn't even protest when A.C. shoved me in a cab.

He got me to the school. The cab ride hurt almost as much as the beating as I jostled around in the back seat, holding my sides. I started to go in and out of consciousness and have only vague memories of him hoisting me up the stairs and then I passed out for real.

When I awoke, Master Yum, A.C.'s teacher, was leaning over me with an intent look on his face, wrapping my ribs. He was a whipcord, crooked-toothed little Korean man who was Grand Master of the ancient Korean style called Hwa Rang Do. It was a very efficient killing art, but it also had a strong healing component. He was an acupuncturist, herbalist and chiropractor. He was applying a lot of foul-smelling ointment on my side under the bandages when he became aware of me looking at him.

"Hwa Rang" I greeted him.

"You rest," he ordered with a little grin. "Two rib cracked."

"You should see the other guy," I said.

"I told Master what happened," A.C. said.

"You spar me when you better," Master Yum said with that little laugh all martial arts masters have that lets you know that they know the punch line. "You need to toughen gut."

"Yes sir." I wouldn't have argued with him if I had a shotgun trained on him and I certainly wasn't going to then and there.

He offered me some herb tea to sip but had to help me to drink it, holding the cup to my lips. "You sleep now; make better."

"Let me call Jill before I go out," I said to A.C. He looked at me with an unsure squint, but when he saw I wouldn't close my eyes until he did, he relented and brought me the cordless phone.

"Sorry to call so late," I said in a weak voice, "but I've got some news that might make up for it." I gave her a cleaned-up version of the events of the night. After I finished, there was a long silence. I could almost see her staring at the phone as if it were a snake that had settled in her hand.

"I'll drop the wallet in the mail tomorrow in Manhattan," I said after a bit, "and it'll all be over."

"Over," she said in echo.

"Yes. This part is over," I said. "Now all we have to do is live."

Jill cried softly at the other end of the line. It continued quietly for a minute, and then I could hear her gather herself up, and she said, "I love you, Eric."

"Love you too, Jill." I handed the phone to A.C.

"They broke the mold when they made you, Eric," he said.

"Before," I said. Then I fell down the rabbit hole and was asleep.

Chapter Twelve

By Friday afternoon when Krystal drove up to spend the last weekend of the faire with me, I could almost walk like a normal person instead of the five-thousand-year-old man and was down to only ten aspirin a day.

"You idiot!" Krystal said with deep sympathy when I told her about what had happened Wednesday in Chinatown. "If you'd told me what you were going to do, I'd have come up and kicked your butt worse than this to stop you."

She gingerly put her arms around my waist as we sat in Frank's Pizza Parlor. We had loaded my gear into her car at my place and then drove to the shrine to the sacred circle for a quick meal before heading up to the faire.

"I really hadn't planned on a beating," I said, "but if I had planned ahead, you would have been my first choice for beater." I smiled and tried to twinkle my eyes. She grunted.

"So what's next?" she asked, doing her best to resist my dynamic charm. "Did you mail the wallet?"

"A.C. did," I said, "from Manhattan and wiped clean of prints. Hardest choice was which letter agency to send it to. We picked the ATF. Figured they could use the good press."

She worked hard at not smiling.

"But what else?" she asked impatiently. "Did the police get them?" She looked so eager, so Peter Pan at that moment, I laughed.

"We once again prevailed on Poppo to check the blotter for the Chinatown precinct," I said. I was working my recitation around

136

consuming four slices; pain or not, I was always up for pizza. "The three men found in the hallway—after they were taken to the hospital—were arrested for breaking and entering, weapons possession and parole violation (Petie had a gun)—and on suspicion."

"Suspicion of what?"

"Oh, gun running, terrorism, etc. It seems my call to the ATF and FBI got results, but Poppo didn't dare ask too many questions. He was suspicious of A.C. making the call as is but let it slide. *The Post* had a little article on a gun smuggling interdiction in Chinatown and the Bronx."

I studied her and saw the same expression as she had that day in Delaware when I'd mentioned the "Free Ireland" pin of Tom's.

"It's over then," she said with a sigh.

"I think so," I said. "I hope so. That part, anyway—the part that brings some sense of justice. It'll never really be over for Jill, or …"

"You."

"Me, I guess," I said quietly.

"You did what needed to be done," she said, trying to boost my confidence.

"I did what I could … what he would have done."

"So now?"

"Now we eat, we drive, we unpack and we screw," I said lustily. "Though not necessarily all in that order."

"At least I won't have to worry about disturbing the campground with my shrieks of lust," she said.

"What do you mean?"

"Your screams of 'ouch' will drown me out!" I'd have taken a swipe at her but it hurt too much to swing my arm. The best I could do was withdraw my startlingly charming stare from her. She didn't seem to notice.

———

The campgrounds, by tradition and convenience, had assumed a true village-like layout, with different groups camping in the same areas, year after year. Royal Knoll, where the jobbed-in actors stayed, was near the phone, showers, and soda machines.

Crafttown, where most of the vendors stayed who had campers with such conveniences as TV and refrigerators; the 'burbs, were way up the hill past some thickets where the more romantically active members of the troupe could have a little more privacy at the cost of a long walk to the privies, and the Stud Farm (named long before I came to the faire I assure you), was near the stables and the province of the fight corps and jousters. Not that all these divisions were by any means rigidly set, but like tends to attract like, and even the outsiders who do the faire like a "stable" structure.

Also by tradition there were two big campfires that attracted various members of the group. The one at Royal Knoll tended to be a "trendy-drinking-gossiping" crowd. The Crafttown fire, more often than not, turned into a drumming circle led by Bob, our joust drummer, and had a distinctly pagan atmosphere. That summer, particularly when Kryss was up, I most often joined the Crafttown bunch.

Very late on Friday night, Krystal and I put in our appearance at the circle. I had only cried "ouch" twice during our afternoon lovemaking in the tent, but she had been admirably restrained in gloating about it.

There were a high number of spouses, mates and "friends" that had come up for this final weekend because Saturday night was the "cast party." It was a final grand farewell to summer.

Lea, the carriage driver for the faire, was with her lover Joan, who had come up for the "last party." At the start of the summer, she was ivory-skinned and red-haired, but now her skin was as brown as a sandal, her hair was almost ash blonde and she had a new tattoo (that she showed to everyone) of a dolphin on her hip. So were Bob the drummer and his wife Alice—as sort of the king and queen of the musicians they hosted the circle. One couple I was surprised to see was Robin and Conn, semi-entwined, as usual.

"Hey guys," I said, "I didn't expect to see you up here, tonight."

As a rule, Mandy and anyone else in their booth came up Saturday morning on the performers' bus that made the trip up from New York

138

and back each day. They always stayed up Saturday night and went back either on the bus or hitched rides with actors Sunday night.

"Oh, Mandy, Jill and Don will come up tomorrow," Robin said, "but Conn wanted us to have, a … well, … to come up early." She was clearly blushing even in the firelight.

"How'd you get here?" I asked.

"I got a loan on a Ranger from a company mate," Conn said. "We have all the gear to take back Monday, anyhow."

He'd been up three of the weekends, and I'd been out to dinner with them and the Swan Company a couple of times, but like most new lovers, they'd kept their focus inward. His beard was fuller, though he'd kept his hair short and he'd filled out in a healthy way in Robin's care.

"You get a professional discount as a mechanic?" I joked. It was what he said he did for a living. It was how he'd gotten his limp, he said, when he'd come backstage to watch preparations.

"A bloody hydraulic jack slipped, and I got wanged in the back," he said. "Did something to the nerve. Doesn't really hurt, just goes dead sometimes. It's not even consistent; now and then, I get in a game of Australian rules football without a limp."

Over the duration of the evening, everyone around the campfire started singing the usual campfire songs, individual and rounds, and we went through every song we knew (including the *Gilligan's Island* theme), ending up at about one a.m. with the traditional Ren faire ender "Happy Trails."

By then, the embers were a faint glow, and the circle had thinned considerably. There was a moment of concern when Mary Anne, from the flower booth, couldn't find her car keys in the dark, but Conn found them with the ever-present little flashlight he wore on his keychain.

"Just call me Flash Gordon," he said, striking a heroic pose.

"G'night, Flash and Dale," I waved goodbye, "watch out you don't step in any Ming on the way to the tent."

Back in my tent, Kryss and I climbed under the covers of the little pallet-bed, pleasantly tired, and she snuggled against me with a smile, albeit gingerly because of my ribs.

I listened to the night sounds of the campgrounds, with someone playing a guitar somewhere softly and a gentle tom-tom sound from the drum circle—more a primal heartbeat than an attempt at music.

I felt Kryss's body heat through the flannel nightshirt she wore and smelled the jasmine scent of her hair shampoo and smiled.

"You know, little Peter," I whispered, "this ain't a bad life."

She just mewed like a cat in agreement and snuggled in a little more.

My last thought before I nodded off to sleep was, "Now you can sleep in peace, Tom."

#

Mornings at the Ren faire lack much of the romance of the nights. It's damp, cold, and a long way to the latrines. That last Saturday morning dawned grey and cold with a promise of rain during the day. My sides ached in a way that told me that, Aspirin or no, I was not going to be jousting that day. I made the decision as I limped my way gingerly up the path to the costume shop. I saw Kelly ambling along and waved over to me. I told him the most embarrassing lie a stuntman can possibly use.

"You fell down some stairs!" he said. He was chewing some tobacco and worked his jaw while he gave me the hairy eyeball.

"Yeah," I worked my best thespian magic to lie, "I hit a slick spot and down I went." He looked at me with one eyebrow cocked, half-Spock, half-Jimmy Stewart, spit his morning chew and said meaningfully

"A-huh."

I'm supposed to be an actor, and his seeing right through me galled me. "Really," I insisted with too much emphasis.

"Better tell the others it was a car accident," he suggested, not the least bit fooled, "More likely they'll buy that." Then, as an afterthought, he gave a gentle smile and added, "It'll be a pleasure to ride against Smitty; he's ready."

Boy, was he ever!

I thought the mad juggler would bounce off the ceiling in his excitement. I'd told him and the other fight corps members the "I'd been in a car accident" lie. There were a lot of "I thought you were walking funny last night" comments and some that snickered they thought it was from Krystal being up, but most seemed to believe me.

Roll call that morning in the costume shop had Dawn Faith (already looped out of her mind) doing her traditional pre-last weekend speech, touching on the usual concerns. "Don't let the fact that it's the last weekend make you think you have license to change scripted scenes or play childish pranks." (Believe you me, no child was ever as devilish with pranks as bored Ren faire actors.) "But above all," she intoned with her screechy Fran Drescher accent, "keep the spirit of the fantasy (pronounced 'feentasee') within you."

We all applauded, then ignored everything she'd said.

I got Courage out of the weapons locker where it and the edged melon-cutting swords were kept (separated from the purely stage swords as a precaution against anyone mistaking them for stage weapons) and went to each of my fight partners throughout the day to make adjustments in our fights necessitated by my injuries.

This wasn't that unusual. Often, fights were "adjusted" for pulled muscles or the like, or when an actor was out altogether with illness or prior commitment. Once that summer, one of my guys got a big film part and had to miss two days (D & B went ballistic), and we had one sprained ankle, which happened during a non-fighting scene.

The changes to the fights I was involved in were not terribly major; we took out two of my flip moves, a major fall became a "drop to the knees and surrender," and we changed two sequences that would torque my ribs too much and were ready to go.

Those who are about to pretend to die salute you!

At the front gate, I saw A.C. and a pretty Korean girl named Nancy, who he was dating. They would stay up for the party later, so I just waved. He pointed to his side with a questioning expression. I nodded to let him know I was okay.

The black leather and velour doublets of the King's Guard that had been so hot in August were now, in the damp weekends of September, just comfortable. Many of the other performers added cloaks and shawls to their attire to cope with the change in the weather. It was starting to be real English weather.

The ominous appearance of the black doublets combined with the physical size of most of the guards (some of the wenches had nicknamed us the "beef patrol") meant that many of the actors came to view us as a real security force. Now, mind you, the faire hired off-duty cops who wore yellow "security" t-shirts and carried guns, but the actors and even the craftspeople knew us and felt more secure having us around for a lot of circumstances.

So if a patron was getting fresh with a wench, forgetting that these were actresses who were playing flirts and tarts, a cry of "What ho!" might go up and, as if by magic, a King's Guard was sure to appear.

In traveling carnivals and circuses, the call for help was "Hey rube!" But "What ho!" kept the illusion going for anyone not directly involved. Usually, the mere presence of a big guy in black was enough to deflect things, at least long enough to find the real security. But sometimes it wasn't.

That Saturday, I had just walked past Mandy's booth, a little late for my next scene, and was waving a hello to the Silver Swan group when I spotted a crowd of bearded men dressed in jeans, leather vests, and motorcycle boots coming down the path.

Nothing unusual in that. Bikers liked the outdoor faire—the wenches, the beer, the joust and the rest. After all, they viewed themselves as knights of the road. Even as lubricated as the biker crowd got, they were usually rowdy in an all-American college boy kind of way. Teddy bears in leather, albeit Teddy bears with fangs.

I went on toward my next scene, which was to greet the Princess Gloria as she stepped from her carriage at the King's Stage, and I was only a few minutes ahead of it on the road. It was a good thing.

I was crossing the meadow near the mud show pit and had just spotted Vita (she was also running late on the way to the same scene) when a high-pitched, urgent "What ho!" came from behind me.

I spun on my heel and took off at a run, my ribs rattling with every step. When I reached the lane, the trouble was clear. Two of the biker group had the carriage horse by its halter, effectively taking control from the driver, who was Lea.

The other bikers had surrounded the open carriage and were suggesting some very un-princess-like activities to her.

I pulled up short, five yards away, and forced myself to walk calmly toward the tableau while scanning for the real security. Of course, none were in sight.

I heard Vita pull up just behind me. "Get the two away from the horse," I whispered without turning around. I kept a big old friendly grin on my face as I moved toward the carriage.

"Got it," she said and vectored off at them. I caught the princess's eye at this point and saw a look of major relief there. I started singing the dirtiest ballad I could think of and sauntered up beside the carriage.

"Four and twenty virgins come down from Inverness, and when they went back home again there were four and twenty less ..."

"Here lads," I said as jovially as possible, "what's all this now?" There were six by the carriage, four on my side, two on the other and two up by the horse. I ignored the last two. They were Vita's problem.

One of the bikers yelled, "Tell'm, Screech!" "Screech" was my height but close to three hundred beer pounds.

"We wanta see if a princess got a curly beaver like a poodle or if her maid combs it out!" The others roared at this as if it were the funniest thing Screech had ever said. Maybe it was.

I laughed long and hard, my eye on Vita, who was joking with the horse holders, making sure they saw whatever little cleavage she had in her tailored doublet at every opportunity. They had already let go of the harness and were talking with her.

Our black doublets made it very easy for these guys to identify with us. "I say laddies," I managed to get out between laughs, "aren't you afraid it'll be a wire-haired terrier, and you might get cut?" This started them laughing again. And now they were focused on me.

"You're okay," Screech said to me in a slurred voice. "Let's duel." He suddenly held a nine-inch, silver shadow-fighting knife in his right hand, double-edged and razor-sharp. The inebriated road ranger jumped back into his idea of an Errol Flynn stance. The other bikers also stepped back to get a good look at the coming action.

"Go ahead, Lea," I said calmly but firmly. She needed no second command; the horses got the carriage away at a brisk walk, now no longer the focus.

"Okay, Knight," I thought, "now you've put your own life in jeopardy. Now what?"

I fell to my knees, threw my hands in the air and blubbered like a true King's Guard. "Spare me life, my lord, for I come from a very long line of cowards. Fear runs in my family. Urine does, too (mostly down me leg). If you promise not to kill me too much, I promise to get you a discount at the guard's brothel. Me sister's not as sick as she used to be. She can handle one more…."

This got them all laughing, Screech loudest of all. He sheathed his knife, came over, and clapped me heartily on the back (boy did that hurt) as he helped me to my feet. I could see that Vita had quietly stepped in to be ready, hand on the sword at her hip. I gave her a look, and she relaxed.

"I dub you Sir Osis of the Liver," Screech said (as if it were an original joke). More idiot laughter from his buddies followed.

"Thank you, sirrah," I said. "Let me show me gratitude and buy you all a round at the tavern on me." They all agreed and headed off to the tavern with my promise to join them "after I change me soiled tights."

When they had gone, Vita nodded to me and took off to the admissions booth to get on the radio to the real security boys. They would meet Screech and the gang at the tavern and "escort" them off the grounds.

I sighed and gingerly touched my ribs. I noticed Conn standing across the road. Then, I noticed he had a white-knuckled grip on his little flashlight.

He saw me looking, dropped it to swing on its chain, and smiled. "Nicely handled, Eric," Conn said. "Good mood management."

"I've been a bouncer," I said. I shivered, more from the pain in my side and adrenaline fatigue than the damp air.

"Still took guts," he said with a sly grin.

"Or lack of brains," I said, "but ultimately I had him outclassed." I made a sudden move with my right hand to grab my broadsword from its scabbard and flourished it. "Mine is bigger," I said with an answering grin. "If he wasn't drunk, he would've figured it out."

Conn laughed. "I get it," he said. "That's not a knife; this is a knife!" in a too-perfect Australian accent that made me wonder just where he had come from.

I made my scene in time and then waddled through the fight with a little wince in my expression the whole time.

I was less than spectacular in my chess game fight; my side, by this time, was giving me a lot of trouble. In my final fight with Kelly, we arranged it so Smitty intervened, and the challenge was between Kelly and the mad juggler (character name Shamus O'Myself). The audience around the board—the regulars, anyway—appreciated the new development. Smitty had a lot of admirers among the regular fairegoers.

After the game, it was time to prepare for the joust. At the stable, all preparations went as normal save that I acted as Smitty's squire, and we added one new element, a very traditional one when a new knight rode the joust.

It happened after Smitty was fully accoutered, and both horses were ready to go.

"Hey," Kelly called from outside the stable, "come out here a minute, will ya, Smitty." His voice sounded urgent. Smitty, myself, and Kelly's second Max came at a run. At the barn door, we froze. Smitty tried to say something, but no sound came out. I just grinned; I'd known it was coming.

Kelly was standing amid a throng of fight corps members, Lea, King Stephen, and some of the other actors not in scenes. In his hands was a pair of simple steel spurs that had been decorated with red ribbons. Stephen looked at me, and I nodded. "Smitty," the king said, "step forward." Smitty moved like a robot to stand before the crowd. "Kneel." He did.

"By the power vested in me by Thespis, Dawn and Barry, and Jack Daniels," Stephen said, accepting one of the edged Patton sabers we used for the melons, "I dub you Sir Smitty of the Shire. Ride honorably and safely and party 'til you drop." He touched the blade to each of Smitty's shoulders and his head. "You kneel as a knave and rise as a knight. Merde!"

Everyone yelled merde.

145

I thought Smitty would cry.

I knew how he felt. When Steve Manley had awarded me my spurs, I had bawled like a little kid. It was the entry into a very exclusive club, one that was connected in many ways to the very history of knighthood going back to the eleventh century or so. Not an official pedigree to be sure, but still a family tree that made us all feel very special.

Kelly and I knelt and tied one spur on each of Smitty's boots.

When we had secured the spurs we stepped away and nodded to all the women who surged forward and covered him with kisses. The faire tradition dictated he leave all the lipstick marks on his face 'til after the joust! He soon looked like he was wearing war paint.

"This is great," Smitty said with a lopsided grin that was barely visible behind the rainbow array of lipstick marks.

"Don't enjoy it too much, hero," Kelly said dryly, "you still have to lose to me today."

Joust time!

The sky turned an ominous grey-black and over the mountains came the faint echoes of thunder. The crowd was a little light, many having already left early in hopes of beating the rain.

Smitty fairly glowed with energy as Whiskey rocketed out onto the field. I jogged out to position as his corner man and waited while Smitty made his circuit. When he pulled up for the bishop's blessing and the ladies' favors, he still had that grin on his face. Then every woman on the stage (some of them "crossing the line" character-wise from the good-guys side) trouped down and each one tied a favor on his arms. He started to look like a Christmas tree.

"This is great!" he whispered as I secured his helmet.

"Just keep your seat, Smitty," I said, "and watch your dismount after the breakaway. Remember to use your arms."

"I'll be okay, Eric," he said, his voice now muffled by the helmet. "Thanks for letting me ride."

146

"I didn't let you do anything, kiddo; you earned it, you're ready. Lose gloriously!"

I scanned the crowd as I trotted to Smitty's lance rack. I spotted A.C. and Nancy, some other people I knew from Medieval Society events, and Conn and Robin in the "no man's land" between the inner and outer ropes. It was an area reserved for staff or their guests.

Robin had little Danny on her lap and both waved. Conn just smiled at me, a little surprise on his face when he saw I wasn't riding, but then they hadn't been at the chess game to see Smitty take the challenge. Beyond them I could see big Dan on the edge of the crowd, and I didn't want to even think what was in his angry mind.

The two riders did an exhibition of skill first, cutting melons out of the air (normally we do that at the earlier "skill joust," but Smitty was so hyped we figured, "What the hell, let him get the whole treatment."

Smitty did great and the first lance-to-lance pass went smoothly.

On the second, Whiskey shied, so Smitty missed Kelly's shield (but so had I plenty of times) and Kelly missed Smitty's. Both signaled to try again, so they did, the timpani drum pounding out a rhythm, and they hit the mark for a beautiful double break.

"Clean," I complimented Smitty when he rode back to get his lance for the last pass where he would take the chest hit. "Stay rooted like that for this one and you're home free." I could hear him breathing heavy in the helmet, mostly from excitement, because his lungs were in better shape than mine ever were.

"Okay," he said. I watched Max for the arm signal. When it came, I yelled, "Go," as I dropped my arm.

The two horses flashed at each other. Smitty dropped his shield arm to open his chest and his lance point dipped a bit. "Compensate!" I said aloud to myself.

Whiskey, feeling Smitty tilt right as the lance dipped, was drifting. Smitty corrected, but a little too late, so Kelly had to reach a bit for it. The lance shattered low on Smitty with a soft *thonk* sound.

Thank God, I thought, *it's still on the vest.*

Smitty dropped his lance and shield and keeled over sideways, his right foot almost catching in the stirrup.

Something was wrong. Smitty hit the ground like a pile of wet laundry. Kelly kept riding to finish his run, unaware that anything was amiss behind him.

All the crowd cheered as at any joust, oblivious to anything wrong or any mishap. Their voices were strangely distorted to me as I started out onto the field.

At the far end of the field, Kelly wheeled about and trotted Crusader back to continue the scene. I had the same cold feeling in my gut I'd had at Tom and Jill's when I saw the ambulance.

I broke into a dead run when Smitty rolled over, and I spotted the piece of lance that had penetrated his body.

Chapter Thirteen

At about seven o'clock Saturday night the heavens opened up and the rain never let up all night. Just as well—the cast party was a perfunctory one, held under the awning of the King's Theater stage. Not much dancing; too much drinking. No one even cracked a smile until I got back from the hospital around nine with the news that Smitty would live.

An eighteen-inch sliver of a balsa wood lance had penetrated through the Kevlar vest and punctured the left lobe of his lung.

"How the hell is that possible," Vita said with anger in her voice. "I thought the vest was bulletproof?"

"Bulletproof," Krystal said. "Most bullets are soft lead with no mass behind them, only velocity."

A.C. nodded. "Vests spread the impact over a wide area, but they are not knife-proof or arrow-proof because of the mass of the blade and shaft. Like the wood sliver."

"But it was balsa," Vita said. She had a couple of beers under her belt and was feeling pretty glum.

"The lances still have to be scored with a carpet knife to make sure they break on cue," Kelly said. "We just should have done it better." He was well into his limit of beers trying hard not to think that Smitty's lying in the hospital was because of something he did or didn't do.

By then, I felt a crushing weight of guilt as well. Our somber little party took place in the barn, along with five or six members of the fight corps and their guests, sitting quietly for a time.

"He'll be okay." Vita voiced all our thoughts. "He has to be."

"Yeah," I said, "he will, but it should have been me."

"You ever worry about dying, Eric?" Tom had asked late one night out of the blue.

We were sitting in the corridor of the Boston Park Plaza Hotel, our backs against the wall during a science fiction convention. Jill was in the Baen Books party talking the ear off a couple of editors with Robin Madden doing commentary and translation. Tom and I were hiding in the hall to stare at nymphets and listen to the relative quiet.

"Excuse me?" I asked.

"During one of your stunts, I mean," Tom elaborated. "Like when you joust or jump out one of those buildings on fire."

"Gee," I said intelligently, "I don't know." I thought a moment and realized I had never really thought about it.

We both just stared down the hallway for a minute at the few party stragglers, some still in costume: Star Trek, Shadow Run, or frathouse chic.

"I don't really think too much about dying," I finally said with great profundity.

Tom nodded and made an "uh-hm" sound deep in his throat.

We continued to stare, listening to the buzz of conversation from the Baen party suite. Every once in a while, we could pick out Jillian's laughter in the room.

"Why?" I asked.

He pointed to the room. "I was dressing today, and I happened to see one of my old stab scars, the one where I twisted and took it on the hip instead of the stomach."

I knew the one he meant. We'd been in locker rooms enough that I'd seen all the eight or so wounds that were souvenirs of his street gang days in Baltimore and Spanish Harlem.

"I've seen it a million times," he continued, "but some reason today I looked at it as if it were the first time I'd seen it and thought about it."

"What about it?"

"Well," Tom continued, swigging from the Fosters can, "when I got it, I was in that mental place that didn't care about living or dying, you know. I was just in the fight to fight." He laughed out loud. "I didn't even think about winning most of the time. I just wanted to fight."

"Must be the Irish in you," I commented.

He regarded me from above the beer can's rim. "Seems to me you've got your share of Irish, or you wouldn't be doing what you're doing for a living."

I nodded. Pretending to hurt and be hurt by people for a living was indeed a way to have all my emotional cake and eat it too. And, of course, you never really have to worry about intentional death.

"At least I'm not out on the streets anymore," he said. "I don't know, man. With Jill in my life and having had time to really think about all the puncture wounds, I couldn't just fight to fight anymore. They say once you really think about death, it always stays with you. You can't re-discover the 'no-mind' that the Zen sword masters talk about."

"That's pretty self-deprecating," I said, "like it's not worth making the effort in staying alive?"

"No, hairbag," Tom said with a jovial smile, "the whole thing is a selfish thing, really. I mean, I die, the putz I'm fighting dies, it doesn't really matter. I've always believed I'd come back anyway." He looked at me real seriously. "Don't you?"

I nodded, though I hadn't thought about reincarnation all that much, except when I held a sword in my hand with that sense that I had done it before. In those moments, it all felt like a continuity beyond my understanding.

He continued. "So like I said, win, lose, it didn't matter as long as I went out with some sense of honor, preferably with steel in my hand so I could make it into Valhalla. But that was all before Jillian. Now …" His voice fell to a whisper. "Now I'd think about leaving her behind—or worse—going into a lifetime without her. That would suck, you know?" He finished his Fosters.

I could see the profundity spell leaving him as his brow un-knitted to prepare for some smart-ass remark. But before it did, he added, "I could fight for her, for you, for anyone or anything I believed in. I could die for her, too, but never like before with no thought but honor. Ya know what I mean?"

I nodded like I understood, but I didn't really.

"Playing the self-blame game, that's a chump's game," A.C. said, responding to my self-recrimination. "Shoulda-woulda-coulda. No. If it were you, you might be dead with your lungs, or if it had been on target instead of low and outside, you would be dead—and woulda-coulda ad nauseam. So can it."

The barn door opened and Jillian and Robin entered, the two of them wrapped in a single clear plastic drop cloth. In the moonlight, they looked like a monster from a *Dr. Who* episode.

"Hey, guys," Robin said as cheerfully as she could. "We come bearing gifts." She held up a big picnic thermos. "Hot cider!"

There was a general murmur of approval and everyone scrambled to find empty cups. Even Kelly poured the last fourth of beer out of his mug to make room for some cheer.

Jillian sat next to me on the hay bale, Krystal on the other side. "Mandy, Don and Conn will be along in a bit," Jill said. "They went to check the integrity of the booth."

I just nodded.

"Are you just worried about Smitty," she ventured, "or indulging in useless guilt?"

"A.C.'s already given me that speech," I said. "Now I'm just achy."

"He's lying," Krystal said, "and he's oozing Catholic guilt."

"I thought so," Jill said. "Tom was the same way, certain that Wounded Knee and the Titanic were his fault when he had one of his moods."

"I'm not in a mood."

"Denial is usually the tip-off," Jill said.

"Stop that." I protested.

"They're always the last to know," Krystal said.

"Stop talking over me."

"That's why we have to help them," Jill added.

"Pick on somebody your own size!" I said. Damn the clever minxes. I wasn't depressed anymore.

"Eric, come here!" Kelly called with some urgency from the back of the barn where our joust gear was kept. I disentangled myself from the ladies. Kelly would be getting our gear together for the last joust of the season on Sunday. I'd have to ride no matter how bad my ribs hurt. I didn't think Max was up to the ground fight at all.

"We can do that in the morning, Kel," I said.

"No," he said, "come here." He had an urgency in his voice that I hadn't heard before.

In one hand, he held a linoleum knife that we used to score the lances—in the other, a balsa-lance tip. "Look at this." He had an intense look on his face that was completely unlike him when he handed me both. I examined the lance, and it seemed perfectly normal, with some pre-scoring already done.

"So?"

"Cut it." He ordered. "Deep."

I did. Or at least, I tried. The hooked knife blade hit a hard spot part way in, and when I switched the angle, I hit the same obstruction.

"Wood knot?" I said.

He shook his head, took the lance from me and whacked it twice on the ground. It should have shattered into thumb-sized slivers. It didn't.

Amongst the shards was one piece about two feet long.

I felt my heart skip a beat. Kelly picked up the piece and, after some effort, cracked it over his knee. He handed me one half. It felt smooth and polished, like it had been shellacked.

"Epoxy, I'll bet," A.C. said from behind me. He glided out of the shadows soundlessly where he had been watching. "That is no mistake of nature."

We broke all the lances. All contained a hard core, the only difference being slight variations of the sliver size. It was not natural.

We sat for some time, absorbing it. Jillian and Krystal joined us.

"Why would someone want to kill Smitty?" Kelly said.

"Not Smitty," Jillian said with a cold, faraway tone that chilled us all. "It's Eric. No one knew Eric wasn't going to joust except Eric, Kelly and Smitty and some of the fight corps. And they didn't know that until right before the joust; this would have had to have been done before."

"And we were with the gear from when the others knew today," Kelly said in a haunted voice. I sat down on an overturned feed bucket.

"It's not over," I said. Jill came to stand by me, gripping my hand in both of hers.

"Who?" A.C. asked.

"It could have been anyone," Kelly said. "Security at this place sucks. Anyone in costume could slip through the campgrounds."

"But not with any assurance of being undiscovered," I said. "Not with the amount of time it took to drill into the lance, pour epoxy and repair the paint. It had to be done at night."

"Then it really could have been anyone," Robin said.

I looked at her. Seated, I was at eye level with her "best assets," so I looked up a little at her face. As I did, I noticed something.

"You've lost your swan," I said. "Did you leave it at the tent?"

She blushed. "No."

She held up her wrist to show a bracelet that was the graceful figure of a long-maned lion with a diamond for its eye. "Conn and I exchanged keepsakes. It was his idea."

Somewhere in my head, a circuit closed. Facts piled up. Things connected.

I knew!

I stood so abruptly I almost knocked Jill over. To no one in particular, I said, "I need proof."

"What?" Jill asked.

"Where's your truck parked?" I asked Robin. She stared at me oddly.

"Back behind the barn and office," she said after a moment. "Conn figured Monday we could drive to the booth with less trouble—"

"I'll bet he did," I interrupted. I was already hurrying to the back door of the barn. The others were calling after me but I ignored them, as I ignored the stinging rain that cut into me when I stepped outside.

The path was graveled out by the office, but it was still pretty muddy. Conn's Ranger was among a dozen staff cars and vans. It was locked. A.C., Kelly, Vita and the others had grabbed coats or wraps and followed me outside.

"Do you have keys to this?" I demanded of Robin.

"No," she said timidly. "Conn's the one who borrowed it from his friend."

"Yeah," I said. I bent down, searching.

"Come back inside," A.C. said. "This is nuts being out here."

I found what I was looking for: a rock the size of my head. I picked it up.

"Have you gone crazy?" A.C. asked. "Put that down."

I stared into his eyes for a moment, then turned and hurled the stone through the passenger window of the Ranger.

Everyone stood silent, stunned for the second it took for me to unlock the door. Then Kelly and A.C. grabbed me.

"Let me go," I said. "I'm not crazy. I have to know, I have to have proof!"

"Proof of what?" It was Krystal talking now. She stood between me and the vehicle, her clothes slicked to her, her head tilted back to stare into my eyes, but blinking furiously to keep out the rain.

"That Conn doctored the lances Friday night!" That stunned them more than the rock through the window.

"That's ... that is insane," Robin managed.

"Is it?" I asked. A.C. and Kelly had released me. I stepped around Kryss and began to search through the Ranger. "Can you tell me he was with you every minute Friday?" I asked her.

"He ... he had to work on the truck, and I was tired."

"So he bedded you down to nap and came up here to work." I pulled a near-empty tube of epoxy and two knitting needle-length pieces of steel from out of a cardboard box in the back of the truck. "With these." Robin staggered a little, and Krystal caught her.

"But why?" Kryss asked.

"He told us ... remember?" I said. My heart was pumping hard, my head aching from the realization as all the pieces fit into place: "All the funny voices, his whole sense of humor, and the cock-and-bull story about the now you see it, now you don't limp."

They all looked at me with suspicion in their eyes.

"Mechanic!" I said. "He said he was a mechanic."

A.C. nodded with understanding, and the others turned to him when he said. "It's underworld slang for a hit man who arranges accidents."

Jillian did a little intake of breath that was amazingly loud, considering the rain was pounding down on us like pebbles, plopping loudly in the puddles at our feet.

I lost any attempt at delicacy as I tore the interior of the truck apart.

"That damn flashlight he always wears should have given it away," I ranted. "It always hangs on his left hip."

"It's just the size of a dan bong," A.C. said quietly.

"It's how Mr. Gunns knew I'd be at Lucky Charms. They were with Jill when I called Mandy's. It's why he cut his hair short after he dyed it, why he had to grow the beard, why he made sure he didn't run into me until he was red, why he faked the limp...."

I found it in a canvas bag on the bottom of the box beneath the copies of the stolen Silver Swan newsletter he'd studied to learn all about Robin. On the top of the stack was a copy of the *New York Post* from June with the picture of me and Vita above the article about the bodega and with my photo circled with the word "hero" written in red ballpoint.

For some reason, that pissed me off more than anything.

And there in the canvas bag was a long denim coat embroidered with patches from different countries on the sleeve and pins of all sorts on the front, including a battered "Free Ireland" pin right over his heart.

"He was gonna add your swan as his next trophy," I said in a voice that cracked. "Conn is Blondie!"

Robin all but fainted. Jill let out a cry of anguish. Kelly and A.C., in unison, said "Damn," like they'd rehearsed it. Vita was more visibly shocked.

I climbed out of the truck and started to run.

I ran as fast and as hard as I could down the gravel path, around the stable, then cut off across the tilt yard.

My sides were on fire with every step, but I really didn't care. "Son of a bitch," I screamed aloud. "You even picked a name to prove we were all chumps!" Then, I saved my breath for running. Don, Mandy and Blondie/Conn were coming up the lane adjacent to the tilt yard, all laughing at one of Conn's jokes. They stopped under a big garden-table umbrella and watched me running across the field.

They didn't react until I cleared the split-rail fence in a dive to slam into Blondie. I clipped Don so he plopped on his butt in the mud.

Blondie and I rolled over twice before we separated. I was in so much pain and filled with so much rage that I was growling like a beast.

Blondie knew "the jig was up." With the instinct of a cornered animal, he got to his feet and booted me hard in the right side. The kick hit my arm first and that took some of the sting out of it.

"Hey!" Don yelled, grabbing at Blondie, who spun and clubbed him down with a swinging fist. Then the killer ran.

He went over the fence and straight back across the muddy tilt yard. He only made it halfway before A.C. and Kelly came bounding over the opposite fence with two-foot wooden dowels in their hands.

Blondie veered off toward the King's Reviewing Stand. He didn't get far before Vita and Rick came over the fence farther down by the stand, effectively heading him off.

He turned to consider running back our way, but I was on my feet and had blurted out who and what he was, so Don and Mandy were prepared to stop him.

Blondie reached the center of the field and just stopped. The action made all of us stop. We stood in a rough circle some twenty feet from him.

"What are you civilized folk gonna do, eh?" he yelled over the downpour. "Turn me over to the bobbies?" He turned slowly to look everyone in the eye directly, stopping at me. "Or are you man enough to try something alone?"

"Why," I asked, "did Tom have to die?"

He laughed, low and bubbly, like a schoolgirl. "Nothing personal. He snitched us to the MI5 boys … your ATF. I was in the pub and spotted the 'suits.' Bad for business if you don't nip that sort of thing in the bud, and business ain't been so good since Gerry Adams become a TV star."

"You weren't SAS or Ulster Constabulary?"

"Not in a while, mate; private entrepreneur." He had a cocky grin as if he were proud of his status.

"And trying to kill me?"

He made a shrugging gesture. "Loose end. You saw me, and you closed me up and, uh … Tommy Gunns's shop. Not to worry, though; I'll start again fresh. Bosnia's hot these days." He looked around again, noting the hesitation of the group to move in. I knew he was working on "mood management" like I had with the bikers. He was sure he had it all in the palm of his hand.

"What's it to be, eh? Clomp on the old darbies?" He held out his hands in a "shackle me" gesture.

The civilized thing would have been to tie 'em up and turn him over to the Feds. But we had what? Some glue, hat pins and my word? Anything we said was hearsay. He'd probably be deported. So much for the legal system.

But there are older laws.

An object flew out of the night and splashed in the mud at my feet. I looked down. It was Courage.

Blondie and I both stared at it. Then, one of the melon-cutting sabres landed at Blondie's feet. We looked up to see Jillian and Robin standing beside A.C. Robin still held the scabbard for the sabre.

Jillian nodded to me. An indomitable look on her face, Robin stared coldly at her lover.

When Blondie finally pulled his gaze away from Robin, there was a look of regret on his face.

"Bleedin' King Arthur is it, then," he said, squatting to pick up the blade. He tested its weight with a practiced hand. "Been a while since Sandhurst," he quipped.

When I bent to pick up Courage, my ribs told me this was indeed a stupid choice. My brain told me it was stupid, too, but I grasped the hilt in my right hand, the scabbard in my left, and pulled hard enough to snap the peace bond away.

I stood and tossed the scabbard and relaxed into an *en garde* stance. The others backed away. We had most of the tilt yard as our killing field.

Now that I stood across from the man who had taken Tom from me, I understood a little what Tim had said to me in that hallway so long ago in Boston. I was very afraid, more afraid than I'd ever been in my entire life, but the anger was there, too. An anger that went to the bone.

I will likely die here, tonight, I thought, *but I will not go alone.*

"Come on," Blondie yelled at me, "ya bloody soddin Mick lover. What are you waiting for?"

I started to laugh suddenly, uncontrollably, as another thought struck me. *My name's Eric Thomas Knight,* I thought. Then, in a voice I still swear had Tom's Baltimore twang, I said aloud, "You killed my brother. Prepare to die!"

Blondie started to laugh at my joke, but the laugh went cold when he saw the cold light in my eyes.

"All right, D'Artagnan, hold onto your tights," he said. "Time to see how they do it without a script."

He attacked with two slashing cuts in a great diagonal X. His form was weak, but the two pounds of steel in his blade were strong enough.

I didn't try to parry. Instead, I tried to retreat, but my foot slipped in the mud, and I went down on my left knee. So much for footwork.

Blondie made an attempt to close on me, but I locked my rapier arm out and stopped him by keeping my point focused on his chest.

My straight rapier and my long arm gave me about a six-inch reach over his sabre, but he was quicker than I was—quicker and fresh from the factory. Still, I was not too well used.

I got to my feet again. We circled to the right, more in a knife-fighter's crouch than any classical sword form. More like the old engravings of Agrippa's rapier crouch.

I didn't feel the rain or the cold or even the ache in my side any more than background static. I felt the sword in my hand and the power of his stare. And I glanced at his blade flashing in the moonlight. That was a mistake.

While I was focused on the blade point, he tossed the handful of wet sand he'd picked up when he crouched to get his blade. It hit me square in the face and blinded me. I panicked for a split second, frantically back-pedaling and slashing with my blade while I tried to clear my eyes.

"*Cha Ryet!*" A.C. yelled in Korean. "Attention!" I stopped trying to see and dropped into the left-arm-sloppy-forms leg trip that I'd learned from Tom. My right foot swept into Blondie's lead leg, and I felt him stumble backward. I blinked my eyes clear in time to see Blondie make it back to his feet. He turned and ran for the grandstand. Vita made a move at him but thought better of facing his sabre bare-handed.

"Stay back!" I yelled. "His soul is mine."

He stopped at that and, with a snarl, turned to face me again. "Mother England got that a while ago, chum." He spit at me. "All I got left is talent." He attacked again furiously. Shoulder, shoulder, head, leg, shoulder. His blade and mine met with sparks and the ringing blades were like Vulcan's forge. As if to answer our fury, peals of thunder and slashes of lightning tore through the sky.

We were as alone on the field as any two warriors had ever been alone in the heat of the battle through the ages. My friends might as well have been a thousand miles away, for his blade could be in me before any of them could stop it.

He was aware of them too, but what his thoughts were I could only guess. Parry, cut, parry. Slash, parry. Hack. There was no art in it. Just fear and strain and reaction. No time for thought.

It might have gone on forever, but Jillian made it end then, at least indirectly. She'd said she was a witch; maybe she was.

What she did was simple: she turned her back. Nothing more. Just turned her back and stood there.

I felt it rather than saw it, for I was a bit too busy to look. Still, I knew it with certainty. Then, one by one, the others did the same. Robin was last. That I clearly saw. So did Blondie. It was as if he had been erased from their lives, and he felt it.

With their gesture, it was as if he and I had been cut loose from everything that was of the earth I'd known. No string of civilization remained in either of us to hold back the beast.

Blondie yelled and cut for my left cheek, right thigh and left side in rapid succession. I parried each as if I knew he was going to make the cut before he did.

On the last parry, as our blades were still in contact, I spun left, whipping my left foot behind me like a rock on a rope in a heel kick. He tried to block with his left hand, but the force of the kick smashed his forearm aside and slammed into the side of his head as he back-pedaled. It was only a glancing blow but it was enough. He fell against the reviewing stand with enough force to jar him back to full consciousness.

He tried to get his sword up then to parry, but I beat it aside with my blade and drove the point of Courage through the center of his chest. I thrust it with so much force that it pinned him like a butterfly.

He dropped his sword and tried to speak, his mouth moving mechanically, but with no sound coming out. I imagined I could feel his still-beating heart slow and pulse as its tissues throbbed around Courage.

There was surprisingly little blood. Just a diluted pink that washed down his body to mix with the mud. I stared into his eyes and could see his awareness slipping away. He did not accuse me with that stare, merely acknowledged my act. But the beast within me was not sated. I accused him with my look and leaving Courage in him, stepped forward to spit in his face and say in Gaelic, "Rot in hell with your mother!"

Then he was gone, dead by my hand, Tom's sword and the justice of the gods.

Epilogue

I don't remember how I got back to my tent, but I remember packing my things and sitting to wait for the police. No police ever came for me though. I fell asleep sitting in the doorway of my tent.

Everything seemed strangely normal when I woke the next morning, the usual sounds of laughter and the smell of coffee were as they had always been. Krystal lay next to me in the bed.

Still in a daze, I made my way to the tilt yard. There was no corpse, no blood and no indication that the night before had been anything but a dream, save for a deep new gouge in the reviewing stand. Everyone prepared for the day as if nothing unusual had happened.

I don't remember most of that day except that A.C. and Kelly were gone, out "sick," which was okay. It was a rainout day anyhow. Robin spent the day in her tent, crying. She cried a lot after that day.

No one ever spoke to me of what they had seen or heard that night. Kryss stayed with me for a week and never spoke of it in so many words. Courage, with its tip broken off, was in its locker safe for the morning parade that never came.

The season finished that day and the autumn was on the greenwood, browning to its annual sleep. Smitty healed by and by and was soon back assisting me, none the worse for the wear.

A month or so later I got a newspaper clipping from an Oswego, New York, paper in an anonymous envelope. It told of an unidentified body found in a deserted stretch of woods with a massive wound to its chest. The police had no clues. I kept the clipping in a pouch around my neck until the next spring.

That was when, a year to the day from Tom's death, we held a Viking funeral for him. We were in Pensacola, Florida. Jill had moved there to be near her folks.

Mandy's Don handcrafted a three-foot dragon ship model, and Mandy made a doll with a black beret on its head, dressed as the Prince of Amber holding a hand-forged miniature of Courage, nicked tip and all to stand in for Tom.

I sent the news clipping with instructions to set it at the feet of Tom's miniature stand-in before the ship was set aflame and set adrift in the gulf. I prayed it would carry him to the Valhalla, where I hoped to join him some day. When people asked me what was in the envelope I just said "Beau Geste," without telling them what it meant. He would know, and that was enough.

As I write this, I'm looking at a picture on my desk of the burning ship. Beside that picture is a photo of Tom and another of Jillian holding their son, Thomas Eric De Dannin. He has my eyes and Tom's smirk.

It helps me sleep at night and eases my conscience.

A lot.

The End … of the beginning.

The book you have just finished reading is fiction but based on fact. My life, in fact, but that life intersected many who have ended up in these pages (albeit somewhat disguised, amalgamated and altered). I wrote the book as part of my process to say goodbye to and honor the memory of the real Tom and his courageous wife. Below is her take on some of the events, which she wrote only recently. They are her words, edited only to change the names. I think you'll see why she inspired so much of what is in this book.

Grief is a Journey

by irishwitch

Sun Dec 11, 2—at 04:39:09 PM

I am writing this for all those who have lost someone this year, and who will celebrate Christmas for the first time without them. This is especially for my Dad, who had to say goodbye to "his girl" on August 13th, after sixty-two years of marriage and sixty-eight as a couple. They met when she was fifteen. They had a wonderful marriage. So, for them, this is the story of my journey through grief after losing my first husband.

At twenty-five, I met Tom, the man who would become my first husband. At twenty-seven, I became his wife. At thirty-four, I became his widow. And I began the journey through my grief.

Even now, twenty-one years later, grief and loss still wash over me like a tsunami, most often when I see his face, perpetually twenty-nine, gazing with that grin from the cover of a paperback novel. He had posed for artists, years before he died and they've been using those photos ever since.

I can understand why.

He was a Celtic archetype come to life, dark-haired, blue-eyed, handsome, with a devil-may-care light in his eyes and the feline grace of the martial artist and fencer he was. When Gregg Press re-released *Nine Princes in Amber*, he posed for Corwin, which was so right because I often think he sprang full-blown from the mind of Science

165

Fiction writer Roger Zelazny, one of his brash, flawed, unforgettable smart-ass heroes. He had dressed as Corwin at SF cons for years, and we staged a mock wedding at a Worldcon for all those who couldn't make the real one. Zelazny gave me away, and we were all dressed as characters from the series. Those books were such an integral part of our life and love story that I buried him in that costume, with a sword in his hand. He went upstairs to talk to the building super, while I stayed to talk with our friend, T.J., his fencing partner. He never came back. And then, suddenly, I KNEW. It felt like getting a medicine ball in the gut. The breath was knocked out of me and I couldn't breathe. Some believe that when two people join their hearts and souls, there is a silver cord that unites them. I swear I felt that cord snap, and I staggered into a chair. I sent T.J. looking for him. And as I waited, alone, I began to sob. I suppose T.J. was gone at most ten minutes. He didn't have to tell me. I KNEW. He had seen the ambulance, and the EMTs were already zipping Tom into a body bag.

When the police showed up at my apartment, they were treating it like a potential homicide or a suicide. I had to answer questions about enemies, about drug use, and listen to an Archie Bunker clone in blue announce, standing two feet away from me that it looked like we had a jumper. The detective was as kind as he could be under the circumstances, but he had to ask those questions, because if it had been a homicide, I would have been the most likely suspect. It probably didn't help that I had gone into the calm of shock because by the time the police arrived, I'd done the first storm of weeping and had already accepted that he was gone.

When the police finally left, T.J. called a friend who packed a suitcase and took me and my cat to her place to stay. Calls were made to friends far and near, and someone volunteered to do the formal identification of Tom's body.

My parents took over burial arrangements. When my landlord announced that I had ten days to vacate since my name wasn't on the lease and he didn't approve of renting to young single women, my friends took care of that too (it was completely illegal but I didn't have the money or strength to take him to court).

Somehow I got through the funeral and the Irish wake, complete with large amounts of alcohol, poetry, songs and the toasts we held after. And then it set in. Reality. He was gone. I would never see his face again. I would never watch him flash that grin and wave from across the street. I would never feel my knees go weak just at the sight of him. I would never again hold him in my arms at night. I was no longer a wife. I was now a widow. I would live the rest of my life without him. I took time off from work to recuperate.

But two weeks wasn't enough. I ended up quitting my job and moving to Florida with my parents.

Before I moved, though, I did something that will undoubtedly shock a lot of you. I asked T.J. to take me to bed. For nine years, my body had known the touch of only one man. I was afraid if I didn't get the *First Time Since Tom Died* out of the way, I'd never be able to touch my sexuality, my femaleness, again. I was afraid I'd freeze inside. I was afraid no one would ever want me again. I was … afraid. It was the right thing for me to do, though for many others, it would be wrong.

Florida was a really BAD choice in many ways. I couldn't get a fulltime job. I was stuck in a family neighborhood surrounded by FAMILIES—something I would never have, because the choice had been taken from me. We were childless by choice, but the possibility was always open to us to change our minds since I hadn't had tubes tied and he'd chosen not to have a vasectomy.

In Florida, I had no friends, or support system. I was living in my parents' home and suddenly, I was given a list of rules to obey, as if I were twelve again. Still, I lived a block from a beach, and I spent my days exercising, riding my bike, swimming. I was in the best shape, ever, and the beach was a healing place for me. The nights were the worst. I would reach for him, and find myself alone. I'd put a pillow over my head, pull the blanket over my head, and sob into the other pillow. I didn't want them to hear me crying. I didn't want to reopen the wound they thought was beginning to heal. I didn't share my grief with them at all.

Finally, one of my friends gave me a verbal kick in the butt and told me to find a con. Grudgingly, I asked and it turned out that one would be there in a few weeks. I attended and met some people, got back in the SCA (Society for Creative Anachronism , a historical re-enactment group) and started going out again. I didn't have a car and hadn't driven in years, but local folks were more than willing to give me a ride to meetings or events. The first event I attended, I cried all the way through it. And nobody minded, once they knew what I was crying about. Tom had also been SCA, and there were moments when I'd turn around, expecting to see him but, of course, he wasn't. C.S. Lewis, who lost his wife to cancer, said that grief is a spiral. Just when you think you have finally moved away from that spot, it curves again, and there you are, in that same place again.

The oddest things triggered memories. I remember seeing the movie *Highlander*. The big fight scene at the end with Connor taking on the Kurgin sent me into torrents of tears. The height difference between Lambert and Clancy Brown was the same as between Tom and T.J.. They had spent the afternoon before Tim died fencing in the schoolyard, Tim with a wooden katana. T.J. with Tom's transition rapier (yes, live steel). I got funny looks from people over that one. Hearing SCA folk singing the music from *Camelot* triggered another flood of tears. We had seen Richard Burton in a revival of *Camelot*, and had both loved the music.

I found life full of "firsts." The first large con without him — really just a gathering of friends. Being on a panel without seeing him grinning at me from the audience. Seeing writer friends who I hadn't seen since his death, who wanted to tell me how much he was missed. Two books were dedicated to him by friends. I cried in the bookstore when I saw them.

I am told I was a picture of grace under pressure. It didn't feel that way. I felt like a maimed creature who would never be whole or right again.

I've said before that the Victorians had a better way of dealing with death than we do. We expect people to slip back into life after having half their heart ripped out. We're supposed to go to work and do our job as if nothing had happened. Mourning veils and black armbands for the first year make sense to me. They tell the world, "This is a crazy person. Don't expect her to behave rationally all the time. She is overwhelmed with pain and sorrow and loss. Give her space to grieve. Give her comfort. Be gentle with her, for she is fragile."

But that isn't how things are today.

You are supposed to just get over it, at least at work. Grief can be a form of paralysis. You can't move. You can't think. You feel as if every step you take, is like wading through quicksand that threatens to pull you down and drown you, but you have no choice. You just have to get through it—somehow.

It is a journey that feels at times like climbing Mount Everest, but it is a journey you MUST undertake because not to is to become in truth the maimed thing you feel yourself to be.

If you don't take the journey, your heart freezes, and you forget how to love, to feel joy, to be alive. You become a zombie, flesh that walks but lacks a soul. Perhaps the worst thing for me was that I stopped writing. I had begun to get a small reputation as a writer of Irish fantasy.

And love and joy and life are the prizes that wait for you at the end.

Now, the words wouldn't come. All my heroes had been Tom in one guise or another—IRA man turned musician, King of the Cats, the hero of two trunk novels. Somehow writing about him when he wasn't there to share the glory felt wrong. I wrote one last story, and then I stopped writing for publication for thirteen years.

A year after Tom's death, my new SCA friends joined me for a memorial service. They had gotten together and built a model Viking long ship. It was perfect, complete with a dragon's head prow, benches for the rowers, water chests, even tiny shields painted with designs. It was done because they cared about me, and felt as if they knew Tom. Friends from all over sent me photographs, letters, drawings, to go into the fire with the ship, so he could have a proper Viking memorial. I cast a circle, presiding as priestess, and we gave him a warrior's sendoff, complete with music he had loved in life.

The year was over. I had gotten through so many firsts. First lovemaking with someone other than him. First Christmas without him. First real relationship with someone other than him. First con with someone other than him as escort. First story in print that he wouldn't see between the covers of a book. The grief, however, wasn't over.

They call it grief work for a reason. It is the hardest work you will ever do—but the most necessary. You MUST let yourself feel it, or you do get sucked in by the quicksand and you do drown. Grieving is exhausting. You cry, and you end up feeling as if you had run a marathon. You put on a game face for everyone else, but then you come home and you sob in the dark. You are angry that the man you loved died and left you alone, and you hate yourself for thinking he had it easy. He just died, and it was over, while YOU are stuck with all this pain, all this loneliness, all this emptiness. You feel guilty for beginning to smile again, for taking pleasure in small things like sunlight dancing on waves or the touch of another man's hand.

I don't think I really began to heal until I met Ben, the man I eventually married. He was married at the time, and he was just my friend—my best friend, the one I could talk to Tom about.

A fellow Wiccan, he didn't think it was strange that sometimes I heard Tim's light baritone calling me "luv" or his hand on my cheek. As he pointed out, I had informed Tom at his funeral, he wasn't supposed to leave me until I was ready.

Ben's marriage ended, and we became more than friends. We became lovers. T.J. flew down to hand him Tom's rapier—Grayswandir, the sword borne by Corwin of Amber, which I had given him upon Tom's death, because he said the sword belonged to my Protector, my Knight. And that was when the journey through grief ended.

I was able to love Ben and to love Tom, without the aching loss that sometimes threatened to choke me. I truly believe that while Dad walked me down the aisle when I married Ben, Tom was on my other side; that he kissed my cheek, and turned and walked back down the aisle with one last flash of that smart-ass grin I loved so much, and faded into the sunlight.

At the reception, my maid of honor sang a song to Ben as my present to him. Joan Baez wrote it for her sister, Mimi Farina, when she remarried. It's called "Sweet Sir Galahad" and it said all that was in my heart. I had two Sir Galahads, and I was blessed. I learned a lot of things from this journey. Here are some of them:

Even a "bad day" is not all that bad if you feel the one you love beside you. Don't worry about your sanity if you see your loved one after they pass over. Most people do. They are with you in spirit as long as you need them. Sometimes that hand you feel on your shoulder is theirs.

Let others help you. Helping you is a gift you can give them. It allows them to heal a bit, too. Don't be afraid to ask for help. People are usually willing to help you, including people you have just met.

The only things you truly regret after you lose a loved one, are the angry, hasty words you wish like hell you could call back—and the times you wish you'd said "I love you," and didn't.

Ben and I get pretty pissed and rather noisy at times, but even if go to bed angry, I always tell him I love him, even if right now I think he's behaving like a horse's ass. And he does the same thing with me.

Love never dies. And there is always enough to go around. Loving someone else does not take away from your love for the one you lost. Broken hearts do mend.

About the Author

Teel James Glenn traveled the world for forty-plus years as a stuntman, swordmaster, storyteller, bodyguard, actor, and haunted house barker before turning to writing.

He has several dozen novels published and his novel *A Cowboy in Carpathia: A Bob Howard Adventure* won best novel 2021 in the Pulp Factory Award. He is also the winner of the 2012 Pulp Ark Award for Best Author.

His short stories have been printed in over two hundred magazines including *Weird Tales, Mystery, Pulp Adventures, Cirsova, Silverblade, Heroic Fantasy, Blazing Adventures* and *Sherlock Holmes Mystery.*

His website is: TheUrbanSwashbuckler.com
Facebook: Teel James Glenn
Bsky: @Teelglenn

Curious about other Crossroad Press books? Stop by our website:
http://crossroadpress.com
We offer quality writing
in digital, audio, and print formats.

Subscribe to our newsletter on the website homepage and receive a
free eBook.